根據多益
最新改制題型

U0098832

NEW TOEIC
新多益

黃金互動16週：進階篇 二版

🎧 附電子朗讀音檔、解析本、模擬試題

李海碩、張秀帆、多益900團隊 編著
Joseph E. Schier 審定

作者介紹

李海碩

- 學歷:
  國立交通大學教育研究所數位學習組碩士

- 經歷:
  臺中市立東山高級中學英語教師
  ETS認證多益英語測驗專業發展工作坊講師
  葳格國際學校總校長

張秀帆

- 學歷:
  國立政治大學英語教學碩士

- 經歷:
  國立政治大學附屬高級中學英語教師
  ETS認證多益英語測驗專業發展工作坊講師

TOEIC 900團隊

專業的多益教材研發及教學顧問團隊，致力於
推廣英語學習。

三民書局

國家圖書館出版品預行編目資料

新多益黃金互動16週：進階篇／李海碩,張秀帆,多益
900團隊編著.－－二版一刷.－－臺北市: 三民，2022
　　面；　　公分.－－（Let's TOEIC）

ISBN 978-957-14-7582-0 （平裝）
1. 多益測驗

805.1895　　　　　　　　　　　　111018401

Let's TOEIC

新多益黃金互動 16 週：進階篇

編 著 者	李海碩、張秀帆、多益 900 團隊
審　　訂	Joseph E. Schier
企劃編輯	陳逸如

發 行 人	劉振強
出 版 者	三民書局股份有限公司
地　　址	臺北市復興北路 386 號 (復北門市)
	臺北市重慶南路一段 61 號 (重南門市)
電　　話	(02)25006600
網　　址	三民網路書店 https://www.sanmin.com.tw

出版日期	初版一刷 2018 年 5 月
	二版一刷 2022 年 11 月
書籍編號	S804200
I S B N	978-957-14-7582-0

三民書局

作者序

你覺得世界上最偉大的發明是什麼呢？我覺得是匯率。

匯率，提供的就是一個計算的基準。而外語證照也是如此。每個外語證照都像是一種匯率，計算著外語能力的程度。不同的證照匯率不同，能換算的方式也不一樣。若沒有外語證照，我要用什麼方式來衡量能力的基準呢？從比較好大學畢業的學生，外語能力就一定會比較好嗎？如果這兩個人英文聽起來都很好，也都很能表現自己，我要如何更快速地知道他們的實力差異呢？外語證照提供了一個絕佳的功能，讓我們可以透過快速、具有公信力的過程，提供一個足以表達外語能力的數字。

本書是臺灣教科書史上於 TOEIC 改版之後的第一套從高中到大專院校都適用的教材，願能以拋磚引玉之心，邀請更多先進共同投入語言檢定教學的領域，讓臺灣的學子在離開校園前，能在履歷上放上具有國際公信力的匯率，為自己的未來與競爭力加分。在此在下也希望特別感謝一路上共同協助的作者張秀帆老師，以及一同努力並提供全面完整支持的三民書局。一家公司願意出版學校教材，就是在社會責任與收益的天秤上，無悔選擇了社會責任的道路。在下極度榮幸能在這個過程中參與並提供所知，期待這套書籍能夠為教育的現場帶來更多的可能性。

李海碩

多益測驗，TOEIC 是 Test of English for International Communication 的縮寫，顧名思義，是一個評量「如何將英文運用在日常生活中」的能力測驗。為了讓英文不再只是一個考試科目，為了讓英文成為實際、可運用的溝通工具，《新多益黃金互動 16 週：進階篇》為老師及學習者量身定做，結合了多益測驗、生活情境、真實語料，成為一本可供教學及自學的多益攻略寶典。藉由書中的教學內容、活動應用及實際試題模擬演練，除了可精進多益成績，更可同時掌握在生活中運用英文的能力，讓英文成為你行遍天下的工具，成為你的能力、你的素養，一舉多得！

十一大情境、實境學習、高頻單字

介紹多益測驗常出現的十一大情境，藉由主題情境衍生出真實狀況、高頻單字、及常見問題，讓學習者能從生活事件中習得單字、片語、對話，就像身歷其境，實際去經歷、體會並應用英文，學習英文不再只是單字之間點與點的學習，而是整個事件的立體情境習得，讓記憶變得容易、學習速度加倍！

單元活動、培養批判思考能力

每單元都有小組或兩人活動的安排，藉由活動討論、問題解決、角色扮演，更精熟每單元的內容，且在活動過程中，試著找出問題、提供解決方法，不再只讀死書，而是藉由自由開放的討論、融會多方回應及建議。讓英文的接觸面更寬廣、更靈活，熟悉更多元的回答方式。當別人問我們 "How are you?"，我們不再只是制式的回答 "I'm fine. Thank you. And you?"

還等什麼？快快跟著《新多益黃金互動 16 週：進階篇》一起達到你人生的英文高峰！

張秀帆

「學生也考多益？」這句話是我在教授多益課程時最常聽到的質疑。事實上，高中生與大專院校生考多益證照有三大好處：一，準備多益考試可同時提高學測英文分數；二，多益的語言認證可全球走透透；三，準備多益考試可提升國際溝通力。然而，要成功習得語言，最重要的是好教材，《新多益黃金互動16週》能精準掌握多益考試的題型及方向，是一套老師和學生都需要的好教材。

兩位編輯者—張秀帆老師以及李海碩老師—皆是美國教育測驗服務社 (ETS) 官方認證的 TOEIC 師資，他們以多年教授多益課程的經驗，編撰出適合教師上課教學及學生準備考試的教材，與市面上的考題解析完全不同。《新多益黃金互動16週》不僅可以提升多益考試成績，更可以讓學生在學習語言時，促進互動及溝通的能力，符合新課綱「溝通、互動」的素養導向。

習得語言、掌握英語優勢，不可僅靠死背單字，最重要的是使用語言，透過同儕間的溝通和互動，才能真正內化英語學習，英語才能真正在國際溝通場合派上用場。《新多益黃金互動16週》教材設計許多單字練習及課堂活動，內容貼近生活實用及考試趨勢，讓學生學習英語不再枯燥乏味，讓學習變得立體且雙向溝通，透過這套教材，老師絕對可以協助學生體驗英語學習的豐富性與趣味性。

臺北市立和平高級中學校長　溫宥基

溝通，從接收訊息開始。隨著國際交流日趨頻繁，有效地溝通便顯得更為重要。在雙向溝通中，最主要的任務即是：接收並理解對方所要傳遞的訊息，然後能依此完整表達自我想法。有鑑於此，若要能夠快速並準確地接收訊息，英語聽讀兩大能力之培養，事不宜遲。

《新多益黃金互動 16 週：進階篇》這本書，以提升學生在生活及職場溝通英語聽讀能力為首要目標，以教師與學生、學生與學生之間互動學習為主，以主題分類的方式，套入新多益測驗之題型內容，並提供題型特色及解題關鍵分析，培養學生對於試題的洞察力。不僅能作為教師課堂教學的得力助手，更能使學生在建立英語聽讀能力上得心應手。

談到這裡，不由得使我回想起一段曾與教師們的談話。我們都是致力於推廣英語教育，也期待所有英語學習者能隨心所欲地使用英語，但在這條路上卻難免有力不從心之時。仔細想想原因，也就是我們身上所擁有的英語能力，以及對英語的熱忱，似乎是無法有效地傳遞給時下年輕學子。我和老師們討論到，如何將畢身所學傳授給學生時，應先激起學生對於學習英語的渴望，進而再去確認其是否確實接收到了預想傳遞之內容，這何嘗不是一種雙向溝通、教學相長呢！

誠摯推薦《新多益黃金互動 16 週：進階篇》，讓有趣的互動教學，引起學生渴望學習的心，相信這本書作為課堂教學得力助手，必能為教師及學生帶來實質上的幫助。

ETS 臺灣區總代理忠欣股份有限公司營運長　吳紹銘

認識 TOEIC

1 TOEIC 是什麼？

TOEIC 的全名為 Test of English for International Communication，亦即國際溝通英語測驗，旨在測驗非英語母語人士在國際職場上的日常英語溝通能力。

2 TOEIC 測驗內容

多益測驗的情境包含一般商務、製造業、金融、企業發展、辦公室、人事、採購、科技、房地產、旅遊、外食、娛樂、保健。為確保不會有利於或不利於特定考生，多益測驗不會出現需要專業知識才能理解的內容，也不會出現如車禍、末期病症、酗酒、犯罪等較為負面的場景。

3 TOEIC 測驗題型

聽力測驗 共 100 題 考試時間為 45 分鐘		閱讀測驗 共 100 題 考試時間為 75 分鐘	
Part 1	Photographs 照片描述題，共計 6 題	Part 5	Incomplete Sentences 句子填空題，共計 30 題
Part 2	Question-Response 問答題，共計 25 題	Part 6	Text Completion 段落填空題，共計 16 題
Part 3	Conversations 對話題，共計 39 題	Part 7	Single Passage Reading 單篇閱讀測驗，共計 29 題
Part 4	Short Talks 短講題，共計 30 題		Multiple Passage Reading 多篇閱讀測驗，共計 25 題 (10 題雙篇閱讀測驗，15 題三篇閱讀測驗)

4 準備 TOEIC 有什麼益處？

1. 增強英文聽力及閱讀能力。
2. 培養資訊整合能力及問題解決能力。
3. 增加對各行各業的探索及對職場文化的認識。
4. 在學習歷程檔案中增加語言能力證明。
5. 提升英文科考試的應試技巧。

1

知道該課主題情境 (Setting) 和焦點題型 (Focus) 後，開始進行暖身活動，熟悉情境。

文中出現的高頻關鍵字彙以粗斜體標記，加強單字記憶。

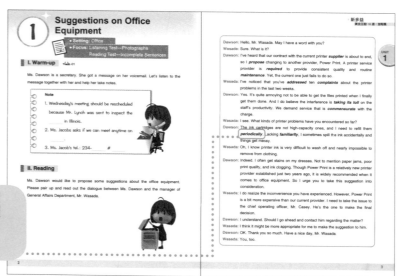

2

進行閱讀任務，透過 TBLT (task-based language teaching) 任務導向的教學方式，自然而然訓練速讀技巧 (skimming & scanning)。

3

認識多益題型及其解題策略，增強聽力測驗或閱讀測驗之應試能力。

4

實戰演練，馬上練習應用剛學到的解題策略。解析本提供解答、聽力腳本及中譯。

🎧 Track
聽力練習的音檔由英、美、澳、加四國口音之錄音員錄製。

5

複習二十個關鍵字彙，
透過該課情境例句掌
握字義。

單字例句皆附音檔，學習單
字時搭配音檔以增強聽力
測驗時對單字的辨認能力。

★★★

單字依難、中、易分級，分
別標記為三顆星、兩顆星、
一顆星。學習者可依程度決
定單字學習的優先順序。

6

學習完一至八單元後，挑戰一回多益模擬試題，
感受考試臨場感。

試題本最後一頁為答案卡。
請注意多益考試時不可在題
本上做記號，僅能在答案卡
作答。

分數對照表提供參考分數；
解析提供逐題詳解及中譯。

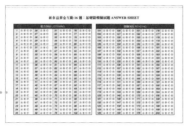

電子朗讀音檔下載

請先輸入網址或掃描 QR code 進入「三民・東大音檔網」

https://elearning.sanmin.com.tw/Voice/

① 輸入本書書名即可找到音檔。請再依提示下載音檔。

② 也可點擊「英文」進入英文專區查找音檔後下載。

③ 若無法順利下載音檔，可至「常見問題」查看相關問題。

④ 若有音檔相關問題，請點擊「聯絡我們」，將盡快為你處理。

⑤ 更多英文新知都在臉書粉絲專頁。

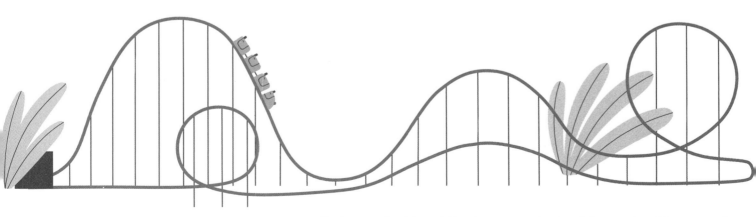

1 Suggestions on Office Equipment

- **Setting:** Office
- **Focus:** Listening Test—Photographs
  - Reading Test—Incomplete Sentences

I. Warm-up Track-01

Ms. Dawson is a secretary. She got a message on her voicemail. Let's listen to the message together with her and help her take notes.

Note

1. Wednesday's meeting should be rescheduled because Mr. Lynch was sent to inspect the _____ in Illinois.

2. Ms. Jacobs asks if we can meet anytime on _____.

3. Ms. Jacob's tel.: 234-_____ # _____

II. Reading

Ms. Dawson would like to propose some suggestions about the office equipment. Please pair up and read out the dialogue between Ms. Dawson and the manager of General Affairs Department, Mr. Wasada.

Dawson: Hello, Mr. Wasada. May I have a word with you?

Wasada: Sure. What is it?

Dawson: I've heard that our contract with the current printer **supplier** is about to end, so I **propose** changing to another provider, Power Print. A printer service provider is **required** to provide consistent quality and routine **maintenance**. Yet, the current one just fails to do so.

Wasada: I've noticed that you've **addressed** ten **complaints** about the printer problems in the last two weeks.

Dawson: Yes. It's quite annoying not to be able to get the files printed when I finally get them done. And I do believe the interference is **taking its toll** on the staff's productivity. We demand service that is **commensurate** with the charge.

Wasada: I see. What kinds of printer problems have you encountered so far?

Dawson: The ink cartridges are not high-capacity ones, and I need to refill them **periodically**. Lacking **familiarity**, I sometimes spill the ink accidentally and things get messy.

Wasada: Oh, I know printer ink is very difficult to wash off and nearly impossible to remove from clothing.

Dawson: Indeed. I often get stains on my dresses. Not to mention paper jams, poor print quality, and ink clogging. Though Power Print is a relatively new printer provider established just two years ago, it is widely recommended when it comes to office equipment. So I urge you to take this suggestion into consideration.

Wasada: I do realize the inconvenience you have experienced. However, Power Print is a bit more expensive than our current provider. I need to take the issue to the chief operating officer, Mr. Casey. He's the one to make the final decision.

Dawson: I understand. Should I go ahead and contact him regarding the matter?

Wasada: I think it might be more appropriate for me to make the suggestion to him.

Dawson: OK. Thank you so much. Have a nice day, Mr. Wasada.

Wasada: You, too.

III. Tasks

After due consideration, Mr. Wasada agreed to Ms. Dawson's suggestion. He is now going to ask the chief operating officer, Mr. Casey, for permission. If you were Mr. Wasada, how would you get your idea across to Mr. Casey? Please finish the following remark that Mr. Wasada is intending to make.

"Mr. Casey, I just met Ms. Dawson, and she told me that. . . .

_____

_____

_____

So she suggests that. . . .

_____

This provider is. . . .

_____

I plan to accept her suggestion, subject to your approval."

IV. Test Tactics

Focus 1: Listening Test—Photographs

新制多益中照片題共六題，每一題一張照片，考生要從聽到的四個選項中選出一個最能描述照片的敘述。此大題是聽力部分最簡易的題型，但選項中可能隱藏誤導考生的陷阱，導致考生失分。

題型特色：三大陷阱分別為「近似音誤導」、「字義誤導」和「句意誤導」。

解題關鍵：聽清楚單字發音、掌握正確字義並理解完整句意。

以右方照片為例，此照片的背景是碼頭，焦點是一艘船，可能的誤導陷阱如下：

1. 近似音誤導

   "There are a duck and a sheep." 為可能的錯誤選項，句中 "duck" [dʌk] 發音近似於碼頭 "dock" [dɑk]，"sheep" [ʃip] 近似於 ship [ʃɪp]，整句聽起來就可能誤以為是 "There are a dock and a ship."

近似音分辨練習 Track-02

兩個單字只有一個母音或子音不同，在語言學中稱為 minimal pair。請試試看以下的 minimal pair 聽力練習，選出你聽到的單字，訓練自己的近似音分辨能力。

( ) 1. (A) mail　　(B) meal　　( ) 5. (A) bean　　(B) bin

( ) 2. (A) sad　　(B) said　　( ) 6. (A) walk　　(B) work

( ) 3. (A) mad　　(B) made　　( ) 7. (A) think　　(B) sink

( ) 4. (A) pain　　(B) pen　　( ) 8. (A) celery　　(B) salary

如果錯了四題以上，可以掃描右方 QR code，至 Sally Jennings 的網站 Speak-Read-Write.com (https://www.speak-read-write.com/minimalpairs. html) 多加訓練自己的聽力喔！

2. 字義誤導

英文單字常一字多義，故準備多益考試時應加強對單字的理解。以左頁照片為例，"The vehicles are being shipped to factories." 就是可能的錯誤選項，句中 "ship" 意為運送，而非船隻。

3. 句意誤導

此類誤導是指選項中雖提及照片上的人事物，但整句句意無法正確描述該照片。以左頁照片為例，"There are many ships in dock." 就是可能的錯誤選項，句中雖提及 "ship" 和 "dock"，但正確的敘述應為 "There is a ship in dock." (有一艘船停泊在碼頭)。

✏ Test tip

近似音誤導中可能出現的不只是單字，也可能是多字的近似音誤導，例如 "He can sell the package." 可能誤聽為 "He canceled the package"。

Focus 2: Reading Test—Incomplete Sentences

句子填空題共 30 題，是多益閱讀部分最簡易的題型，測驗單字、詞類變化及文法概念。

題型特色：文法難度最高僅至「與事實相反的假設語氣」。

解題關鍵：掌握假設語氣的基本概念。

假設語氣的基本概念是只要表達「與事實相反」就要讓時態往過去的方向推一格，用法整理如下：

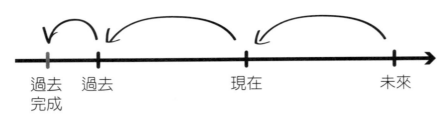

過去完成　過去　　　現在　　　　未來

	條件子句 (if . . .)	主要子句
一般假設	從未來往過去推一格，變成表達一般狀況的「現在式」	根據語意調整，未來狀況就使用未來式
與現在事實相反的假設	從現在往過去推一格，變成「過去式」	should / would / could / might 加上原形動詞
與過去事實相反的假設	從過去再推一格，變成「過去完成式」	should / would / could / might 加上完成式

以下方試題為例：

1. If the revenue were better, we _____ a lot more possibilities.

   (A) capture

   (B) could capture

   (C) could have captured

   (D) captured

條件子句為過去式，表示是與現在事實相反，主要子句應為 should, would, could, might 等過去式助動詞搭配原形動詞，故答案為 B。

2. If John _____ three months earlier, he would have received much less pension.

   (A) retired

   (B) retires

   (C) had retired

   (D) would retire

主要子句為過去式助動詞 would 搭配完成式，表示是與過去事實相反，條件子句應為過去完成式，故答案為 C。

V. Learn by Doing   🎧 Track-03

A. 請聆聽 1–6 題，選出最能描述照片的答案。

1.

4.

2.

5.

3.

6.

B. 請完成 7-10 題，確認自己是否掌握假設語氣。

7. If the manager used effective communication **strategies**, the employees _____
   more efficiently.
   (A) work
   (B) can work
   (C) worked
   (D) could work

8. This project would have **solidified** if the company _____ enough funds.
   (A) gets
   (B) got
   (C) had got
   (D) has got

9. If Graysen _____ this challenging task, his **supervisor** will assign him to the
   headquarters.
   (A) completes
   (B) complete
   (C) completed
   (D) will complete

10. Owen Corporation _____ higher sales if they had **launched** their products a
    month earlier.
    (A) might achieve
    (B) might have achieved
    (C) may achieve
    (D) may have achieved

VI. Vocabulary Track-04

1. **equipment** [ɪˋkwɪpmənt] n. 裝備；設備

The company has budgeted for office **equipment** renewal.

公司編制了預算來更新辦公室設備。

2. **inspect** [ɪnˋspɛkt] v. 檢查；審視

The executive director from the headquarters will be **inspecting** our branch this afternoon.　今天下午，總公司的執行董事將要來視察我們的分店。

3. **at short notice** phr. 接到臨時通知；在短時間內

Mr. Wales finished his work and left for Osaka **at short notice**.

Wales 先生一接到通知立即完成工作，前往大阪。

4. **inconvenience** [ˌɪnkənˋvinɪəns] n. 不便

We are going to have the **inconvenience** of not being able to use the staff lounge for a week.　我們將會因為一個星期無法使用員工休息室而有些不方便。

5. **supplier** [səˋplaɪɚ] n. 供應商

Our company is a large **supplier** of office equipment.

我們公司是一家辦公室設備的大供應商。

6. **propose** [prəˋpoz] v. 提議；建議

Larry **proposes** that we postpone the meeting until next Monday.

Larry 提議我們將會議延後到下週一。

7. **require** [rɪˋkwaɪr] v. 需要

This document **requires** a few minor adjustments before you hand it to the chairman.　這份文件在交給董事長之前需要微調。

8. maintenance [ˈmentənəns] n. 維護；保養

Later, there will be a **maintenance** shutdown. Please take the stairs instead of the elevator. 稍後將進行維護停機，請改走樓梯不要搭電梯。

9. address [əˈdrɛs] v. 對…說話；提出言論

The staff are encouraged to **address** any questions and comments at the monthly meeting. 員工被鼓勵在月會上提出任何疑問和想法。

10. complaint [kəmˈplent] n. 抱怨；投訴

We've received quite a lot of **complaints** about an employee on your team.
我們接到許多對你們團隊中一位職員的抱怨。

11. take its toll phr. 造成損失；造成不良影響

The malfunctions of the office equipment have **taken their toll** on the employees' performance and productivity.
辦公設備的故障已經影響了員工的工作表現和生產力。

12. commensurate [kəˈmɛnʃə,ret] adj. (大小、程度) 對應的

Ms. Gibson's job is **commensurate** with her relevant experience, qualifications, and leadership. Gibson 小姐的職位與她的相關經驗、資格和領導能力相稱。

13. periodically [ˌpɪrɪˈɑdɪkl̩ɪ] adv. 定期地

The office software on the employees' computers is updated **periodically**.
員工電腦裡的文書軟體會被定期更新。

14. familiarity [fə,mɪlɪˈærətɪ] n. 熟悉；精通

Familiarity with English and office software is required for the position.
精通英語和文書軟體是這份工作所需的條件。

UNIT
1

15. revenue [`rɛvə,nju] n. 收益

The social networking service earned advertising **revenue** of over $9 billion in the second quarter of the year.

這家社群網路公司在今年第二季度獲得超過九十億美元的廣告營收。

16. pension [`pɛnʃən] n. 退休金

Penelope retired from the electronics firm with a good **pension**.

Penelope 從這家電子公司退休，得到優厚的退休金。

17. strategy [`strætədʒɪ] n. 策略

They have spent three hours discussing the **strategies** to increase the market share.　他們已經花了三小時討論增加市佔率的方法。

18. solidify [sə`lɪdə,faɪ] v. 使確定；鞏固

Employees' support for the company's Internet use policy is **solidifying**.

員工對於公司網路使用政策的支持日益鞏固。

19. supervisor [`supɚ,vaɪzɚ] n. 主管；監督者

After serious consideration, the **supervisor** finally accepted Levi's proposal.

謹慎考慮過後，主管最終接受 Levi 的提案。

20. launch [lɔntʃ] v. 發表，推出 ★★★

The company will **launch** new products by the end of this year.

公司將在年底前推出新產品。

2 Bank Services

● Setting: Finance
● Focus: Reading Test—Single Passage Reading

I. Warm-up

Layla works at C&B Bank. She received a notice this morning in her office. Let's read it together with her.

C&B

NOTICE OF POLICY ADJUSTMENTS

We have made some adjustments to how we conduct banking business. Please follow the new policy:

- Clients have to be the owner or **authorized** signer on the **account** in which they want to make a **deposit**.
- At least one form of government issued ID is **required** when a client wants to make cash deposits / **withdrawals**.
- At least two forms of government issued ID are required when a client wants to **cash** / deposit **checks**.
- Clients must sign on the reverse side of the check before it is **presented**.
- We do not **permit** the cashing of international checks. Clients must first deposit them and then may **withdraw** the money after a minimum of 12 days.

These requirements should be enforced by all of our branches as of today. Adjustments like these help us combat criminal activities such as money laundering.

Deal with cash and checks with **discretion**. Let's make C&B a bank that people can **count on**.

After reading the notice, Layla meets her first client today. This client wants to cash an international check. If you were Layla, what would you say? Discuss with your partner and complete Layla's words below.

How can I cash this international check?

Sorry. You can't _____ _____ here, but you can _____ to your account at C&B. You can then withdraw the money after _____ days. And don't forget to sign on the reverse side of the check. You also need to show _____ forms of ID when you deposit it and show _____ form of ID when withdrawing the money.

II. Reading

C&B Bank are going to **acquire** another bank. They send all their clients the following letter. Let's read it and summarize the main points.

C&B

To clients, current and future,

We are excited to announce that C&B bank has reached a **definitive** agreement with WestWorld Bank under which we will acquire WestWorld Bank and all its 246 branches around the U.S.

WestWorld Bank is the second largest independent bank in Washington, with total assets **appraised** at nearly $1.5 billion, and deposits of $1.1 billion. The combination will definitely provide natural market extension for both institutions.

As a result of the **acquisition**, the one million WestWorld Bank customers will transfer to C&B Bank, along with some 4,500 staff members currently employed in the branches. This is a powerful partnership, built on the highly regarded **reputation** of WestWorld Bank and the comprehensive resources of C&B Bank. After the combination, C&B Bank will have a network of 588 branches and are going to become one of the four largest banks of America.

We'll still stay true to our firm belief—of committing to putting clients first. Our first priority will always be to maintain the strong client service reputation that has differentiated C&B from other banks for over 27 years.

Let us all look forward to a brighter and more promising future.

Sincerely,

Kerry T. White

CEO, C&B Bank

III. Tasks

Discuss with your partner what information you get from the letter and check the boxes below. You can also write down the information that isn't listed.

☐ the total assets of C&B Bank

☐ the total assets of WestWorld Bank

☐ the branch number of C&B Bank after the combination

☐ the branch number of WestWorld Bank

☐ the number of staff members of C&B Bank

☐ the number of staff members of WestWorld Bank

☐ the four largest banks in the U.S.

☐ _____

☐ _____

IV. Test Tactics

Focus: Reading Test—Single Passage Reading

新制多益的閱讀部分中，單篇閱讀測驗共有 29 題。總共十篇文章，每篇約二至四題。

題型特色：在新制多益中，單篇閱讀題組中含有篇章結構題型，測驗考生是否能將一完整
　　　　　句子歸回文章合適的位置。

解題關鍵：先分析該句重點，再根據文章中四個空格的前後文進行快速判讀。

以下方試題為例：

UNIT
2

Nashua Free Press

(May 27)－A spokeswoman for Yankee Roasters announced yesterday that it will open at least six new locations throughout New England over the next six months. [1] Nashua's third location will open next week and a second location in Lynn, Massachusetts will open before the end of next month. The regional restaurant chain has gained a good reputation in the twelve years since it opened through its genuine regional cuisine, personal service and reasonable prices. [2]

The rapid growth has caught many observers by surprise. It has recently surpassed Hampshire Grille as the largest New Hampshire-based restaurant chain by sales. When it opens its first location in Providence, Rhode Island in the fall, it will have a presence in each of the six New England states. [3] "We have been very happy with our growth over the past five years," said General Manager Jake Labrie. "We offer genuine New England fare, which draws in locals and tourists alike." When asked if there are any plans to expand outside of New England, Labrie said, "I don't see that happening any time in the near future. [4] I don't think there will be much of a market for this outside the borders of New England."

Other locations will be opened in Augusta, Maine; Burlington, Vermont; and Storrs, Connecticut.

1. In which of the positions marked [1], [2], [3], and [4] does the following sentence best belong?

"We are a New England business serving New England food."

(A) [1]

(B) [2]

(C) [3]

(D) [4]

解題步驟如下圖：

分析句意
"We are a New England business serving New England food."

句意重點
1. 表達口吻：第一人稱 (we)　　2. 關鍵字：“New England”

判讀 [1]、[2]、[3]、[4] 前後文

前後文判讀重點：
1. 表達口吻：[1]、[2] 前後文為第三人稱新聞敘述口吻，[3]、[4] 前後文出現第一人稱的發言引文
2. 關鍵字：[4] 後文出現 “New England”

回答問題

回答問題：(D) [4]

"I don't see that happening any time in the near future. [4] I don't think there will be much of a market for this outside the borders of New England."

V. Learn by Doing

請用下方試題練習前後文判讀技巧。

Questions 1–4 refer to the following letter.

Valleyhill Youth Club
65 Buford Highway
Doraville, GA 30340

December 15
Enrique Bascunana, Director
Community Development Department
City of Doraville

Dear Mr. Bascunana,

We here at the Valleyhill Youth Club are very grateful for the support that has been given to us by you personally as well as by the City of Doraville. Our programs have allowed many children to have a place to go after school and on weekends that they might not have had otherwise. [1] It has also been a great thing for the kids of our very diverse community to come together and participate in fun activities with one another.

We now have so many children, and we are having problems with space and other resources. [2] There is a large piece of unused land owned by the city government between our property and the river. If we would be able to acquire that property, we would be able to expand our programs further and build a soccer field, which many of our children would love to see. [3]

If the city government could permit us to use the land to build a soccer field, that would be the best option for us. [4] It would enable us to accommodate more children and give them a safe environment to get some activities after school.

Again, we thank the Community Development Department for its long record of support for what we do here and hope that they can assist us to further serve the children of our community.

Regards,

Joseph Liu
Director of Youth Activities
Valleyhill Youth Club

---

1. Why is Mr. Liu writing to Mr. Bascunana?

   (A) To ask for more money for the Valleyhill Youth Club

   (B) To talk about the diverse students at their program

   (C) To ask for the use of land owned by the City of Doraville

   (D) To get permission to build a soccer field on his property

2. What is indicated about Doraville?

   (A) There are children of many different ethnic backgrounds.

   (B) The children go home immediately after school.

   (C) The City of Doraville does not care about the children.

   (D) The children are all white and English-speaking.

3. In which of the positions marked [1], [2], [3], and [4] does the following sentence best belong?

   "However, we don't have the **_financial_** resources to purchase such a large piece of land."

   (A) [1]

   (B) [2]

   (C) [3]

   (D) [4]

4. What will Valleyhill Youth Club most likely do if they get the permission?

   (A) Invest in property

   (B) Build a soccer field

   (C) Expand their office

   (D) Buy a piece of land

 Test tip

進行篇章結構題的句意分析及前後文判讀時，可從以下幾個方向入手：

1. 表達口吻：適用於文章含有不同人稱敘述的情況。

2. 重複字：重複字常為關鍵訊息。

3. 指示代名詞、指示形容詞及定冠詞：當文句出現 this、that、these、those、such 或定冠詞 the，表示訊息是已知的舊訊息，極有可能在前文已出現。

4. 轉折語 (transitional words)：當文句出現 therefore、moreover、however 等轉承語氣的字眼時，表示該句和前文具有較特殊而明顯的脈絡關係。因為判斷轉承語氣較花時間，必須確實瞭解前後文的完整文意，建議判讀時先使用 1.、2.、3. 來鎖定可能的選項，最後有需要才使用 4. 來判斷正確答案。

VI. Vocabulary Track-05

---

1. **finance** [ˈfaɪnæns] n. 財務；金融

   Jaxon is the **finance** director of a life insurance company.

   Jaxon 是一家人壽保險公司的財務長。

---

2. **authorize** [ˈɔθəˌraɪz] v. 授權；批准

   The finance chief is the authorized signer on this business account; namely she has

   been **authorized** to make withdrawals from this account for the company.　財務長

   是這個公司帳戶的授權簽署人，也就是說她已被授予替公司從這個帳戶提款的權限。

---

3. **account** [əˈkaʊnt] n. 帳戶

   Nora needs to draw some money from her **account**.

   Nora 需要從她的帳戶提款。

---

4. **deposit** [dɪˈpɑzɪt] n. 存款

   To open an account in our bank, one needs to make a minimum **deposit** of $25.

   要在我們銀行開戶，最少需存入二十五美元。

---

5. **require** [rɪˈkwaɪr] v. 需要

   A second identification and a salary slip are **required** if you want to apply for a loan.

   如果要申請貸款，需要第二身份證明文件和薪資單。

---

6. **withdrawal** [wɪðˈdrɔəl] n. 提款

   Hannah makes a **withdrawal** from her account once a month.

   Hannah 每月從她的帳戶提款一次。

---

7. **cash** [kæʃ] v. 兌現

   In the US, some convenience stores and supermarkets provide check **cashing**

   services.　在美國，有些便利商店和超市提供兌現支票的服務。

UNIT
2

8. check [tʃɛk] n. 支票

Victoria deposited the **check** I made out to her in her account.

Victoria 將我開給她的支票存進帳戶。

---

9. present [prɪ`zɛnt] v. 提出

Before **presenting** the loan application to the bank, please make sure you have filled in all the required information.

向銀行提出貸款申請書之前，請確定所有必填資訊都填寫完畢。

---

10. permit [pɚ`mɪt] v. 許可

The manager of R&D plans to use the latest technology, if the company's financial conditions **permit**.　如果公司的財務狀況允許，研發部經理計畫使用這項最新的技術。

---

11. withdraw [wɪð`drɔ] v. 提款

Without enough money in hand, Ryan went to the ATM to **withdraw** some cash.

Ryan 手邊的錢不夠，所以去自動櫃員機提取一些現金。

---

12. discretion [dɪ`skrɛʃən] n. 謹慎

After experiencing the failure in the last investment, SUK Bank now deals with investments with great **discretion**.

自從經歷上次投資失利，SUK 銀行現在對於投資非常謹慎。

---

13. count on phr. 信賴；仰賴

Mr. Roberts is a financial consultant you can **count on**.

Roberts 先生是一位你可以信賴的財務顧問。

---

14. acquire [ə`kwaɪr] v. 取得；購得

Ms. Jones **acquired** her first financial corporation in 1988, and now she owns 12 corporations around the country.

1988 年 Jones 小姐購得她第一間金融公司，現在她在國內共擁有十二間公司。

15. **definitive** [dɪˋfɪnətɪv] adj. 最終的

These two financial corporations finally reached a **definitive** agreement on sharing their resources.　這兩間金融公司最終取得共識要共享他們的資源。

16. **appraise** [əˋprez] v. 估計；估價

The total assets of that bankrupt food company were **appraised** at twenty-eight million dollars.　那間倒閉的食品公司的總資產估計有兩千八百萬元。

17. **acquisition** [ˌækwəˋzɪʃən] n. 獲得；收購

The company's founder believes that their **acquisition** of Rock Monday will generate huge profits.

這家公司的創辦人相信他們對 Rock Monday 的收購將帶來豐厚的收益。

18. **reputation** [ˌrɛpjəˋteʃən] n. 聲望，名聲

Stealing customer lists and selling them to the competitors has totally ruined the general manager's **reputation**.

偷竊客戶名單並賣給競爭對手已經完全毀了總經理的名聲。

19. **maintain** [menˋten] v. 維持；保持

It is difficult to **maintain** a good reputation, yet it is easy to ruin one.

要維持好名聲很困難，但要毀掉它很容易。

20. **financial** [faɪˋnænʃəl] adj. 財務的；金融的 ★★★

The consulting firm is struggling with serious **financial** problems.

這家顧問公司正努力解決嚴重的財務問題。

UNIT **2**

Computer Repair

- **Setting:** Technology
- **Focus:** Listening Test—Short Talks

Lisa is a **salesperson** at BestMart. The sales manager is making an announcement about their annual sale. Listen to the announcement and help Lisa take notes.

Note

1. Prize: a _____ _____ for two in Tahiti. (must get!!!)

2. Advantages of David Tech. computers: a long lasting _____, long term durability, light weight, _____ capability, and a foldable keyboard. (able to function like a _____)

3. Sell one David Tech laptop, get _____. Sell one domestic appliance, get _____.

4. offer up to _____ discounts

5. If merchandise is _____, the points will be deducted.

II. Reading

Ben bought a new computer at BestMart; however, problems with the computer keep popping up. He made a call to a customer service hotline and left a message. Please read out the message now.

I used to think very highly of Feather Computer, but that changed after I bought a Feather laptop 4322, 15 inches. I bought it at BestMart on August 2nd, which is only four months ago. That means my computer is still under the one-year limited warranty. I've called the customer service hotline several times, but they either put me on hold or transferred me to different departments. Finally, a **consultant** told me it was a software issue. How come he was sure it was a software issue when he didn't even take a look at my computer?

My computer keeps making a loud noise, and it oftentimes **shuts down** for no reason. Moreover, the **wireless** network keeps kicking me off. And, whenever I get the luck not to be kicked off, my computer becomes super slow. It takes five minutes to **load** a web page on average. So, basically, the computer is now a useless metal box. In my case, I don't see Feather Computer standing behind its products or warranties. I'm very disappointed.

I'm gonna send a computer problem report form to the customer service email box. I demand that you resolve the problems, rather than throwing the problems back at me. Please contact me ASAP. My phone number is 0912-123-123. I hope you'll try hard to win a customer's heart back.

Ben downloaded a computer problem report form. Let's help him fill out the form.

Computer Problem Report Form

- -

We are terribly sorry for the problems you encountered. Please fill out this form and email it to our customer service email box. We'll reply to you as soon as we receive your report.

1. **Your Name:** _____ *Ben Warren* _____

2. **Date of purchase:** _____

3. **Computer series**

   PC: (1) KingKung--☐a) KingKung 550 ☐b) KingKung 600 ☐c) KingKung 650

             (2) Ocean   --☐a) Ocean V1.0   ☐b) Ocean V2.0

   laptop: (1) 3220   ☐12"   ☐13"   ☐14"   ☐15"   ☐17"

            (2) 4100   ☐12"   ☐13"   ☐14"   ☐15"   ☐17"

            (3) 4322   ☐12"   ☐13"   ☐14"   ☐15"   ☐17"

            (4) 5199   ☐12"   ☐13"   ☐14"   ☐15"   ☐17"

   tablet: (1) OriginW ☐9.7"   ☐12.9"

            (2) OriginX ☐9.7"   ☐12.9"

4. **What is the problem?** (Please check the box next to the problem you encounter.)

   ☐ 1. Can't connect a printer to the computer

   ☐ 2. Blue Screen of Death

   ☐ 3. The computer is too slow.

   ☐ 4. The computer shuts down on its own.

   ☐ 5. Can't connect to the Internet

   ☐ 6. The computer makes noises.

   ☐ 7. The computer can't **recognize** a USB **device**.

   ☐ 8. The computer hardware doesn't work properly.

   ☐ 9. Any other. Please **specify**: _____

5. **Other requests or suggestions:** *Please contact me as soon as possible.* _____

6. **If you wish the Customers Service representative to contact you, please leave your email address or phone number**: _____ .

IV. Test Tactics Track-07

Focus: Listening Test—Short Talks

新制多益的簡短獨白共有 30 題。總共十篇獨白。

題型特色：含有需要搭配圖表資訊才能作答的題型。

解題關鍵：先閱讀題目，掌握問題關鍵，再聽取關鍵訊息，搭配圖表作答。

以下方試題為例：

	Discounted price	Original price
Adult tickets	$ 50	$ 100
Children's tickets		$ 70

Look at the graphic. What is the price of the sold-out tickets?

(A) $50

(B) $80

(C) $70

(D) $100

解題步驟如下圖：

1 速讀題目，掌握題目關鍵字 "sold-out"

2 掌握聽力要點「哪種票已售完」
聽取關鍵訊息 "The discounted adult tickets have been sold out."

3 搭配圖表訊息，可知答案為 (A)

	Discounted price
Adult tickets	$ 50

下列聽力測驗每三題為一題組，請聽取關鍵訊息後搭配圖表作答。

Items	Discount
Wearable Tech	40%
Headphones	50%
Keyboards	37%
Mice	50%
Hard Drives	12%

Food/drink	Price
Coke	$5.50
Mineral Water	$4.50
Vegetarian Lunch Box	$7.00
Fruit Salad	$8.35

1. Why is the store having a sale?

   (A) They are closing down.

   (B) They are promoting a grand opening.

   (C) They are rolling out new products.

   (D) They are celebrating an anniversary.

2. Look at the graphic. What is the discount on keyboards?

   (A) 32%

   (B) 37%

   (C) 40%

   (D) 42%

3. Where can customers see the list of discounts?

   (A) On their website

   (B) At the front door

   (C) In the local newspaper

   (D) At the counter

4. Where is the train heading?

   (A) Sydney

   (B) Melbourne

   (C) Toowoomba

   (D) Brisbane

5. Look at the graphic. How much does the vegetarian lunch box cost today?

   (A) $4.50

   (B) $8.35

   (C) $6.00

   (D) $7.00

6. What does the speaker say the train staff will do later on?

   (A) Serve food and beverages

   (B) Do an emergency drill

   (C) Check the passengers' tickets

   (D) Make an announcement

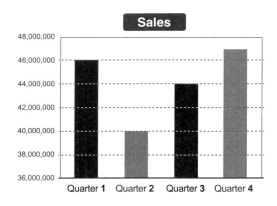

Sales

UNIT
3

7. What kind of company does the speaker most likely work at?

   (A) A real estate company

   (B) A furniture company

   (C) A cell phone company

   (D) A hardware company

8. Look at the graphic. How much did the company make from sales due to new marketing projects?

   (A) $46 million

   (B) $40 million

   (C) $44 million

   (D) $47 million

9. What does the company hope for in the next quarter?

   (A) A 15% growth in sales

   (B) A 10% growth in sales

   (C) A 15% growth in advertising revenue

   (D) A 10% growth in advertising revenue

Name of award	Awarded to
Gold Stevie Award	Environmentally friendly companies
Silver Stevie Award	Highly profitable companies
Mega Business Award	Strongly growing companies
Bronze Stevie Award	Successful business launches

10. Look at the graphic. Which category of business does Wintek belong to?

   (A) Environmentally friendly companies

   (B) Highly profitable companies

   (C) Strongly growing companies

   (D) Successfully launched businesses

11. What was the CEO's main purpose of establishing the company?

   (A) To protect the environment

   (B) To make loads of money

   (C) To compete with other car companies

   (D) To create fuels derived from natural substances

12. Why is the company creating new fuels?

   (A) To make huge profits

   (B) To reduce global warming

   (C) To appeal to customers

   (D) To learn more about environmental pollution

VI. Vocabulary Track-09

1. **salesperson** [ˋselzpɝ.sn̩] n. 銷售員；業務員　複 salespeople

   Good **salespeople** understand their products' value and their customers' needs.

   好的銷售員瞭解產品的價值及顧客的需求。

2. **technological** [͵tɛknəˋlɑdʒɪkl̩] adj. 技術的；有關科技的

   "Mechanical-muscle" machines have caused a trend of **technological** unemployment.　機械勞力已經導致一股科技性失業潮。

3. **line** [laɪn] n. 商品類型；產品系列

   X&M Inc. is going to roll out new **lines** of laptops in December.

   X&M 公司將在十二月推出新系列的筆記型電腦。

4. **last** [læst] v. 持續；維持品質

   The cheaper tablet is said to **last** only a year and a half, while the more expensive one can last about three years.

   較便宜的這臺平板電腦據說只能使用一年半，較貴的那臺能持續使用約三年。

5. **durability** [͵djʊrəˋbɪlətɪ] n. 耐用性

   All the electronic products from our company have been tested for one-year **durability**.　我們公司所有的電子商品都經過一年耐用性的測試。

6. **capable** [ˋkepəbl̩] adj. 有能力的

   You will find **capable** and devoted technicians at this computer repair shop.

   你在這家電腦維修店會找到能力好又敬業的技師。

7. **function** [ˋfʌŋkʃən] v. 運轉；具有…功能 ★★★

   The copy machine isn't **functioning** properly today.

   影印機今天運作不正常。

8. tablet [`tæblɪt] n. 平板電腦

Anthony likes to watch movies and play games on his **tablet**.

Anthony 喜歡用平板電腦看電影和玩遊戲。

9. deduct [dɪ`dʌkt] v. 扣除；減除

Kim got her sales points **deducted**, for a customer returned the cell phone he purchased from Kim yesterday.

Kim 的銷售點數被扣除了，因為昨天有個顧客將向 Kim 購買的手機退貨了。

10. consultant [kən`sʌltn̩t] n. 顧問

Benjamin is a computer **consultant**. He can help solve your computer problems.

Benjamin 是一位電腦顧問，他可以幫你解決你的電腦問題。

11. shut down phr. 停止運轉；關閉

The computer often **shuts down** by itself. Maybe it has been infected with a virus.

這臺電腦常自動關機，可能是中毒了。

12. wireless [`waɪrlɪs] adj. 無線的

The **wireless** mouse can connect to a computer through a USB receiver.

這個無線滑鼠能透過 USB 接頭的訊號接收器與電腦連接。

13. load [lod] v. 載入；安裝

It takes the infected computer two minutes to **load** a single web page.

這臺中毒的電腦光載入一個網頁就需要兩分鐘。

14. recognize [`rɛkəg,naɪz] v. 認出；認可

The new system fails to **recognize** my fingerprint, so I can't get access to my own computer.　新的系統無法辨識我的指紋，因此我無法使用我的電腦。

15. device [dɪ`vaɪs] n. 儀器

Eight hundred dollars is the total price for the following **devices**: a computer, a gaming mouse, and a Bluetooth keyboard.

總價八百元包含以下所有設備：一臺電腦、一個電競滑鼠及一個藍牙鍵盤。

---

16. specify [`spɛsə,faɪ] v. 明確指出

The employees can't **specify** the problems they encounter, which has caused great confusion for the maintenance personnel.

員工無法明確指出他們遇到的問題，以致於維修部人員相當困惑。

---

17. request [rɪ`kwɛst] n. 要求

At the annual conference, the Department of Technology made a **request** for financial support to upgrade their equipment.

在年度會議上，科技部門要求財務支援以更新他們的設備。

---

18. bargain [`bɑrgən] n. 便宜貨

The digital camera is a real **bargain** at that price.

這臺數位相機以這樣的價格來說算是便宜貨。

---

19. pamphlet [`pæmflɪt] n. 摺頁；小冊子

The **pamphlet** is aimed at helping salespeople introduce the new product to their clients.　這個摺頁旨在幫助業務員將這項新產品介紹給客戶。

---

20. quarter [`kwɔrtɚ] n. 季度

The marketing manager expects an increase in sales in the second **quarter** of the year.　行銷部經理預期今年第二季銷售額的增長。

A Business Expo and a Workshop

4

I. Warm-up

Gillian got an email from her boss, Mr. Cole. The email is marked as highly important!

Let's read it together with Gillian now.

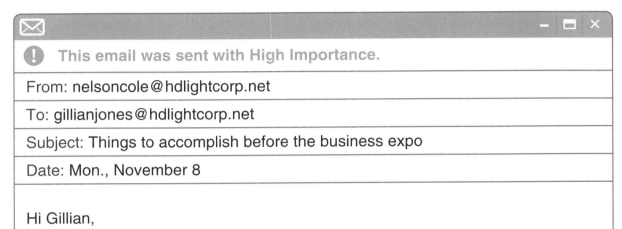

⚠ **This email was sent with High Importance.**

From: nelsoncole@hdlightcorp.net

To: gillianjones@hdlightcorp.net

Subject: Things to accomplish before the business expo

Date: Mon., November 8

Hi Gillian,

We are going to attend Virginia Business Expo. This is a huge event for our company, and hopefully, through this exposition, we'll get more orders and contracts. Here's something important that I need you to do—preparing a brief report on all our LED lighting products and **incorporate** in the report a list of our current clients. Please send me the report by Thursday noon, **at the latest**. And please accomplish the following two tasks before November 20th:

(1) Meet with the Design Department to talk about designing new page **layouts** of our flyers. Please send me the new design for final approval before you send it to the printer.

(2) Order two boxes of business cards for the general manager and the chief marketing officer. They are the representatives of our company at that expo.

Let me know if you need assistance. I'll assign an assistant to you if necessary. I know you have always been **diligent** and **dependable**. Keep up the good work!

Nelson Cole

Marketing Manager

Gillian is planning her schedule. Yet, she finds it difficult to get her priorities straight. Discuss with your classmates and fill in the boxes below with 1 (the most urgent) to 7 (the least urgent).

☐ Prepare a report on LED lighting products

☐ Incorporate a list of current clients

☐ Discuss how to design new page layouts of flyers

☐ Send the new design of flyers to Mr. Cole

☐ Send the final version to the printer

☐ Order business cards

☐ Consider the need of assistance

II. Reading

Mr. Cole is being sent by the chief marketing officer to attend a workshop. Read the workshop *agenda* below and guess which speeches Mr. Cole would like to listen to.

Workshop for Young Entrepreneurs and Marketing Supervisors

Wednesday, December 1	Vast Convention Center	9:00 AM to 4:00 PM

09:00 AM–10:00 AM — Meet the *Entrepreneur Panel*!

10:00 AM–12:00 PM — Workshop *Session* #1

Room 1 Six Steps to Increase Your Productivity (by Strongwill Business Experts)
––Want to expand your business? You need more products! If you want your business to start flourishing, you just can't miss this speech!

Room 2 How to Start My Business (by HighQ Business Consulting Firm)
––Want to be your own boss? Want to be a successful entrepreneur? Want to know more about preparing funds and choosing a business location? Come to us!

Room 3 How to Make Money Online
(by Jack Johnson, a successful young Internet entrepreneur)
––Want to be a rock star in running an Internet enterprise? The 20-year-old young man will share with you his own successful experience. You'll be sorry if you miss out on this great opportunity!

12:00 PM–2:00 PM — Lunch

2:00 PM–4:00 PM —Workshop Session #2

Room 1 Earn 6 Figures a Year as an Internet Marketing Genius (by NetKing)
–– You wouldn't believe how easy it can be to make money on the Net.

Give yourself a chance to know all the tricks and to be the king of the Net.

Room 2 How to Find Great Merchandise to Sell (by Elizabeth Jr. Wu)

—— What products should you purchase wholesale? Will the product be a big hit? Purchasing is a science!

Room 3 Four Secrets a Marketing Person Must Master (by Janet Jane)

—— Master effective strategies to trade properly and keep you on the right side of the market! Come get *motivated* and learn more about marketing!

Workshop tickets are available at *registration*.

The tickets can get you free drinks at Penny's bar from 4:00–6:00 PM.

III. Tasks

Which speeches would be most suitable and most helpful for Mr. Cole? Choose one speech in the morning and one speech in the afternoon for him. Then share your reasons with your classmates.

In the morning: ☐ Room 1: Six Steps to Increase Your Productivity

☐ Room 2: How to Start My Business

☐ Room 3: How to Make Money Online

In the afternoon: ☐ Room 1: Earn 6 Figures a Year as an Internet Marketing Genius

☐ Room 2: How to Find Great Merchandise to Sell

☐ Room 3: Four Secrets a Marketing Person Must Master

IV. Test Tactics

Focus: Reading Test—Double Passage Reading

新制多益的雙篇閱讀測驗共有 10 題。總共兩題組，每題組 5 題。

題型特色：文體多為應用文，如書信、表格、公告、廣告、網頁資訊等。

解題關鍵：1.掌握兩篇文章各自的目的 (purpose)，如促銷、通知、詢問、數據呈現等，從而進行資訊整合。

2.留意細節中的關鍵資訊，如電子郵件中的收件人、寄件人、主旨、寄信時間、附加檔案、表格外圍的小字體註記等。

3.留意文章及題目中的關鍵訊息可能以同義字或「換句話說 (paraphrase)」的方式呈現。

以下方試題為例：

Questions 1–5 refer to the following email and list.

To: Jason White, Warehouse Manager
From: Alisha Stone
Date: July 2
Subject: Problems in the Warehouse Department

Dear Jason,

It has come to my attention that there have been a number of problems in the Warehouse Department over the past few months. I am certain that you are aware of them. There have been too many instances in recent months of running out of products, leading to unacceptable wait times for delivery of orders and double-deliveries, which adds to our shipping costs.

I understand that it is sometimes difficult to predict the *flow* of certain products. Thus, we are going to invest in a state-of-the-art *inventory* tracking system to help your department maintain real-time inventories. You will also have greater flexibility in determining stock levels in the future, especially for seasonal items or other items which have irregular order patterns.

If you have any other ideas that can help your department be more *efficient* to serve our customers' needs, do not hesitate to run them by me.

Alisha Stone

Inventory List

Date: July 2

Product	Current Inventory	Orders		
		April	May	June
Air Conditioners	12	2	4	10
Heaters	4	2	1	0
Microwave Ovens	6	15	14	16
Toasters	152	81	86	76
Blenders	143	76	81	79

*Data recorded by Accounting & Inventory Tracking System (traditional version)

1. What is the purpose of the email?

   (A) To ask why the Warehouse Department is not doing its job well

   (B) To order heaters and air conditioners

   (C) To address issues associated with deliveries

   (D) To check the date of deliveries

2. What might be Alisha Stone's position in the company?

   (A) Warehouse Manager

   (B) General Manager

   (C) Warehouse Associate

   (D) Accounting Manager

UNIT
4

3. Which product will most likely benefit from flexibility in stocking levels?

   (A) Air conditioners

   (B) Microwave ovens

   (C) Toasters

   (D) Blenders

4. According to the list, which product does the company need to stock up on?

   (A) Toasters

   (B) Heaters

   (C) Air conditioners

   (D) Microwave ovens

5. In the email, the word "state-of-the-art" in paragraph 2, line 2, is closest in meaning to

   (A) smart

   (B) beautiful

   (C) advanced

   (D) simple

解題步驟如下表：

	使用解題技巧	掌握文章關鍵訊息	回答問題
Q1	1. 留意細節 (電子郵件主旨) 2. 留意同義字 (problems 同 issues)	Subject: Problems in the Warehouse Department	(C)
Q2	留意細節 (收件人、寄件人)	To: Jason White, Warehouse Manager From: Alisha Stone ▼ 從信件口吻推斷寄件人位階高於收件人，即高於 "Warehouse Manager"。	(B)
Q3	兩篇文章資訊整合	資訊連結題 You will also have greater flexibility in determining stock levels in the future, especially for seasonal items or other items which have irregular order patterns. (信件第二段第三句) ▼ 表格中最明顯呈現 "irregular order patterns" 的產品為冷氣。	(A)
Q4	留意細節 (表格上的日期)	Date: July 2 ▼ 庫存清單上的日期為七月初，而微波爐目前的庫存量低於其六月的訂單量，故可推知微波爐需要再進貨才可以應付七月可能的訂單量。	(D)
Q5	1. 兩篇文章資訊整合 2. 留意細節 (表格外圍的小字體註記)	資訊連結題 . . . we are going to invest in a state-of-the-art inventory tracking system to help your department maintain real-time inventories. (信件第二段第二句) ▼	(C)

表格外註記顯示目前使用的系統為 "traditional version"，可推斷即將投資的系統不是傳統的舊系統，故可推知 "state-of-the art" 的意思應近於 "advanced"(先進的)。

V. Learn by Doing

請完成下方試題，練習雙篇應用文的閱讀技巧。

Questions 1–5 refer to the following web page and email.

Somerville School District

Somerville, North Dakota

Job Vacancies

Middle School Social Studies Teacher: Social Studies Teacher needed for grades 6–8. Must have state ***certification*** and at least five years teaching experience.

Information Technology Assistant: IT Assistant needed for a local elementary school. A bachelor's degree in a related field is required. Must be ***proficient*** in a variety of software programs. A basic ability to work with hardware is also essential. Primary duty will be to assist teachers with software use.

Office Assistant: English Department of Central High School needs an assistant for the department office. A bachelor's degree is required. Responsibilities include providing support to teachers and ***administrative*** support to the department office. Having ***previously*** worked in a school would be beneficial but not required.

Please email your résumé and cover letter to: May Alcott, hiring@somervilleschools.edu

---

UNIT
4

To: hiring@somervilleschools.edu
From: rodrigo425@yakoo.com
Date: May 21
Subject: Middle school social studies teacher position
Attachment: RodrigoLacasa.doc; Cert.pdf; LOR1.pdf; LOR2.pdf

Dear Ms. Alcott,

Good day. My name is Rodrigo Lacasa. I am writing to **inquire** about the middle school social studies teacher position. I am certified in the state of South Dakota for grade 6–12 social studies teaching and am looking to move to North Dakota. I have taught for more than ten years, including two years at an American school in the Philippines.

I understand that I still need to gain North Dakota certification, and I expect to get it by the end of this year. I have attached my résumé, a scanned copy of my South Dakota certificate, and two letters of recommendation.

Teaching social studies has always been my passion. I believe history and social sciences can play a pivotal role in influencing how students see the world and themselves. I would appreciate it if you would give me this chance.

Sincerely,
Rodrigo Lacasa

1. Who is the web page **intended** for?

   (A) Workers in the school district

   (B) People looking for a job in the school district

   (C) People working at an American school in the Philippines

   (D) The news media

2. What is indicated about Mr. Lacasa?

   (A) He did not send a cover letter.

   (B) He does not have any teaching certificate.

   (C) He has taught for more than twelve years.

   (D) He has not been well qualified for the job he applied for.

3. How long does Mr. Lacasa think he still needs to get the state certification?

(A) About one month

(B) About three months

(C) About five months

(D) About seven months

4. If you have basic computer skills and just graduated with a bachelor's degree in sociology, which job are you qualified for?

(A) Middle School Social Studies Teacher

(B) Information Technology Assistant

(C) Office Assistant

(D) All of the above

UNIT
4

5. In the email, the word "pivotal" in paragraph 3, line 2, is closest in meaning to

(A) similar

(B) crucial

(C) famous

(D) typical

VI. Vocabulary Track-10

---

1. **incorporate** [ɪn`kɔrpə,ret] v. 納入

   In our final design, we've **incorporated** the suggestions from five other experts.

   我們最終的設計版本納入了其他五個專家的建議。

---

2. **at the latest** phr. 最遲，最晚

   Joel needs to get his proposal finished by Thursday **at the latest**.

   Joel 最晚需要在星期四前完成他的提案。

---

3. **layout** [`le,aʊt] n. 版面設計

   Please inform the design department that this page **layout** should be redesigned since there are new products to present.

   請通知設計部門此頁面需要重新設計，因為有新產品要發表。

---

4. **diligent** [`dɪlədʒənt] adj. 勤奮的

   My crew is extremely **diligent** in preparing next Monday's presentation.

   我的團隊非常勤奮地準備下週一的發表。

---

5. **dependable** [dɪ`pɛndəbl̩] adj. 可靠的

   The manager should assign a **dependable** person to substitute for you while you are on a business trip to Italy.

   當你去義大利出差的時候，經理應該會指派一個可靠的人來代替你。

---

6. **agenda** [ə`dʒɛndə] n. 議程

   There will be plenty of items on the **agenda** for the next regular meeting.

   將有許多事項會被排入下次例會的議程。

7. **entrepreneur** [ˌɑntrəprəˋnɝ] n. 創業家；企業家

To be a successful **entrepreneur**, one has to not only know how to run a business but also know how to motivate people.

要成為成功的企業家，不但要懂得如何經營事業，還要懂得如何激勵人心。

8. **panel** [ˋpænḷ] n. 專家小組

This seminar is hosted by a **panel** of financial experts.

這場研討會是由財經專家小組所主持。

9. **session** [ˋsɛʃən] n. 時段

The question and answer **session** will be conducted at the end of the product launch event. 問答時間會在產品發布會的最後進行。

UNIT
4

10. **motivate** [ˋmotəˌvet] v. 激勵；激發

Savannah hopes to **motivate** her staff to be more productive.

Savannah 希望激勵她的員工提高工作效率。

11. **registration** [ˌrɛdʒɪˋstreʃən] n. 登記；註冊；登記處

You can get the catalogue of our products at **registration**.

你可以在登記處拿到我們商品的目錄。

12. **flow** [flo] n. 持續的供應，流通

The retailer uses a state-of-the-art system to manage the **flow** of its goods.

這家零售商使用最先進的系統來管理商品的流通。

13. **inventory** [ˋɪnvənˌtɔrɪ] n. 存貨，庫存

The store keeps a large **inventory** of domestic appliances in their warehouse.

這家店在他們的倉庫裡囤積大量的家電存貨。

14. efficient [ɪ`fɪʃənt] adj. 效率高的

This position requires someone who is experienced and **efficient**.

這個職位需要一個有經驗且效率高的人。

---

15. certification [ˌsɝtəfə`keʃən] n. 認證

Please enclose **certification** and three references with your application.

請隨申請表附上資格證明及三份推薦函。

---

16. proficient [prə`fɪʃənt] adj. 熟練的；精通的

Brayden is **proficient** in management and organization skills.

Brayden 精通管理和組織技巧。

---

17. administrative [əd`mɪnəˌstretɪv] adj. 行政的

Lincoln's responsibilities are mainly **administrative**, including organizing meetings, modifying documents, and filing.

Lincoln 的職責主要是行政方面的，包括安排會議、修改文件和歸檔。

---

18. previously [`privɪəslɪ] adv. 先前地

Aaron was **previously** employed as an investment advisor by Golden Corp.

Aaron 之前在 Golden 公司擔任投資顧問的工作。

---

19. inquire [ɪn`kwaɪr] v. 詢問

The R&D Manager called the sales department to **inquire** about the sales records.

研發部經理打電話給業務部門詢問銷售紀錄。

---

20. intend [ɪn`tɛnd] v. 打算；設計給…

The cell phone with a large screen is **intended** for the elderly.

這款大螢幕的手機是為年長者所設計的。

5 Plan a Trip to Greece

● **Setting:** Travel
● **Focus:** Listening Test—Question-Response

I. Warm-up Track-11

Noah is planning to travel to Greece with his colleague. He is now calling the front desk of a hotel to book a room. Please listen to their telephone conversation.

According to the conversation and the information below, how much will Noah need to pay for the accommodations?

Room type	Price	
Single Room ◇ 1 single bed	$ 105	**All rooms are equipped with:** ■ Desk ■ Phone ■ TV ■ Hairdryer ■ Mini bar ■ Safe ■ Air conditioner ■ Complimentary Wi-Fi
Twin Room ◇ 2 beds	$ 125	
Deluxe Room ◇ 1 double bed	$ 148	
Executive Room ◇ 1 double bed & 1 single bed	$ 185	

Noah needs to pay $ _____ .

II. Reading

After the confirmation of the accommodations, Noah and his colleague Wyatt start planning their trip. Please pair up and read out the dialogue between them.

Wyatt: Hey, Noah. Do you have time to discuss our itinerary now?

Noah: Sure. I'm thinking about going to Rafina on the first day.

Wyatt: What a coincidence! Rafina happens to be my top choice to visit!

Noah: Wow! Wonderful! There are lots of restaurants there, **specializing** in fried seafood—fried shark with garlic sauce, small fried fish, and fried squid.

Wyatt: Sounds so delicious! We both happen to be seafood lovers. Perfect!

Noah: And I found that the most popular restaurant there is Agoni Grammi. We can have lunch and a couple of **refreshing** beers there.

Wyatt: Then we can spend the afternoon relaxing by the harbor, watching lots of fishing boats going in and out. We can also stroll along the long beach nearby.

Noah: Great! Then we can order the hotel **shuttle** to take us back, and our first day can **culminate** in the dinner buffet offered by the hotel.

Wyatt: As for the second day, I'd like to visit the temple of Poseidon at Sounion. It is part of the fantastic cultural **heritage** of Greece.

Noah: Good idea. I know that in ancient times, Athenian sailors thought of the temple as the last sign of **civilization** they could see when they sailed away from Athens, and the first sign of civilization on their return journey.

Wyatt: Wow, interesting! There seem to be many stories about the place. Do you know Byron the poet carved his name into a marble column of the temple?

Noah: Really? That's a funny **anecdote**! Maybe it was carved by some naughty tourist. Anyway, we can go find the inscription and take a picture there.

Wyatt: Then we can go to Schinias. It's a beautiful beach.

Noah: My travel book says it has a pine forest and that the waters are **generally** clean.

Wyatt: And most importantly, it is warm. We can swim there. But there might also be a lot of people by the beach because July is **high season**.

Noah: It's OK. We can find somewhere to swim.

Wyatt: Oh! Let's stop right here. I need to go back to work now.

Noah: Sure. Talk to you later.

III. Tasks

Now Noah is recording their itinerary in his notebook. Please help him record it according to the dialogue you just read.

Greece Trip

July 13-16

Time	Activity
	Day 1
10:30 AM	Arrive in Athens
11:00 AM	Check in at Phoenix Hotel
11:40 AM-12:00 PM	Take the shuttle to _____
12:00 PM-14:00 PM	Have lunch at Agoni Grammi
14:00 PM-17:00 PM	_____
17:00 PM-17:20 PM	Take the _____ back to Phoenix Hotel
17:20 PM-19:20 PM	Enjoy the dinner buffet at the hotel
	Day 2
8:00 AM-10:00 AM	Go to _____ by bus
10:00 AM-12:00 PM	_____
12:00 PM-14:00 PM	Have lunch
14:00-15:30	Go to Schinias by taxi
15:30-18:30	Walk along the beach and _____

The Temple of Poseidon

IV. Test Tactics

Focus: Listening Test－Question-Response

新制多益中聽力部份的應答問題共 25 題，題目數量減少且回答變短，考生需要更專注。

題型特色：正確選項可能為非典型應答。乍聽之下似是答非所問，其實是較間接的回應。

解題關鍵：理解層面不可停留在字面語意，而需完整理解說話情境。

以 "Are you driving to the office?" 為例，此句字面上是詢問對方是不是要開車去辦公室，典型的直接應答可能為 "Yes, I am." 或 "No, I'm driving home."，然而此問句的目的可能是希望對方如果順路可載自己一起到辦公室，因此對方的非典型應答可為 "Would you like a ride?"

非典型應答練習

請按以下步驟進行非典型應答的預測練習，訓練自己靈活應對說話情境的能力：

1. 聽問句，將問句聽寫在表格上 Question 欄位。

2. 兩人一組想出至少兩個可能的非典型答句，寫在表格上 Possible Indirect Responses 欄位。

3. 聽選項，並在最適當的選項上劃記。

4. 對答案，將正確答案寫在 Answer 欄位，並比較正確答案是否接近自己的預測。

1. （範例）	**Question**	Are there any vacancies at your hotel?	Track-12
	Possible Indirect Responses	Sorry, we're booked out. What type of room would you like to book?	
	Answer	Ⓐ Ⓑ Ⓒ I am afraid you need to try the one across the road.	
2.	**Question**		Track-13
	Possible Indirect Responses		
	Answer	Ⓐ Ⓑ Ⓒ	Track-14
3.	**Question**		Track-15
	Possible Indirect Responses		
	Answer	Ⓐ Ⓑ Ⓒ	Track-16

V. Learn by Doing Track-17

請聽以下 1–8 題，在最適當的選項上劃記。

1. Mark your answer on your answer sheet.
2. Mark your answer on your answer sheet.
3. Mark your answer on your answer sheet.
4. Mark your answer on your answer sheet.
5. Mark your answer on your answer sheet.
6. Mark your answer on your answer sheet.
7. Mark your answer on your answer sheet.
8. Mark your answer on your answer sheet.

1	Ⓐ Ⓑ Ⓒ	5	Ⓐ Ⓑ Ⓒ
2	Ⓐ Ⓑ Ⓒ	6	Ⓐ Ⓑ Ⓒ
3	Ⓐ Ⓑ Ⓒ	7	Ⓐ Ⓑ Ⓒ
4	Ⓐ Ⓑ Ⓒ	8	Ⓐ Ⓑ Ⓒ

UNIT
5

VI. Vocabulary Track-18

1. vacancy [ˋvekənsɪ] n. 缺空；空房 ★★★

Try another hotel. There are no **vacancies** at this one.

試試其他的旅館，這間已經沒有空房了。

2. spacious [ˋspeʃəs] adj. 寬敞的 ★★★

The sea-view rooms in R&N Resort have a spectacular view, yet they are not very **spacious**.　R&N 渡假中心的海景房可以觀看壯麗的景色，但空間不是非常寬敞。

3. adjustment [əˋdʒʌstmənt] n. 調整；適應 ★★★

We need to make an **adjustment** to our itinerary because I found that the gondola is closed for maintenance on Mondays.

我們需要調整一下行程，因為我發現纜車每週一為了維護會停止營運。

4. in advance phr. 事前，預先 ★★★

Paradise Resort is very popular. You need to make a reservation and pay a deposit **in advance**.　Paradise 渡假中心非常受歡迎，你必須提前預約並預付訂金。

5. **complimentary** [ˌkɑmpləˈmɛntərɪ] adj. 贈送的，免費的 ★★★

The hotel offers delicious **complimentary** breakfast.

這家旅館免費附贈好吃的早餐。

---

6. **specialize** [ˈspɛʃəlˌaɪz] v. 專攻；專門從事 ★★★

Kennedy took us to a fancy restaurant which **specializes** in seafood and wine.

Kennedy 帶我們去一間專賣海鮮和葡萄酒的豪華餐廳。

---

7. **refreshing** [rɪˈfrɛʃɪŋ] adj. 耳目一新的；提神的 ★★★

After a long walk in the sun, Grace drank a bottle of **refreshing** fruit juice.

在大太陽底下走了許久後，Grace 喝了一瓶沁涼提神的果汁。

---

8. **shuttle** [ˈʃʌtl] n. 接駁車 ★★★

The **shuttle** can take you from the hotel to the beach.

接駁車能將你從飯店載到海灘。

---

9. **culminate** [ˈkʌləˌnet] v. 以⋯告終；達到最高點 ★★★

Our trip will **culminate** in a visit to the original store of the coffeehouse chain.

我們的旅程將會在拜訪連鎖咖啡店的創始店後結束。

---

10. **heritage** [ˈhɛrətɪdʒ] n. 遺產 ★★★

These temples are considered part of the cultural **heritage** of this country.

這些廟宇被認為是這個國家文化遺產的一部分。

---

11. **civilization** [ˌsɪvələˈzeʃən] n. 文明 ★★★

Cameron went to Athens to learn more about the **civilizations** of ancient Greece.

Cameron 到雅典以增加對古希臘文明的瞭解。

---

12. **anecdote** [ˈænɪkˌdot] n. 軼事；趣聞 ★★★

There are **anecdotes** about some historical figures in the brochure.

小冊子裡有一些歷史人物的趣聞。

13. generally [ˋdʒɛnərəlɪ] adv. 普遍地；通常

People in that small town are **generally** friendly and hospitable.

那個小鎮的人們通常都非常友善和好客。

14. high season [ˌhaɪˋsizn̩] n. 旅遊旺季

Hotel rates are usually higher during **high season**.

旅館價位在旅遊旺季時通常較高。

15. access [ˋæksɛs] n. 使用機會

Guests who stay in the deluxe rooms have **access** to all the amenities and facilities at our hotel.　住在豪華房的賓客可以使用我們旅館所有的設施和設備。

16. cancellation [ˌkænsl̩ˋeʃən] n. 取消

Many of the hotel room bookings are subject to **cancellation** because of the blizzard.　許多旅館預約都因暴風雪而取消。

17. pedestrian [pəˋdɛstrɪən] n. 行人

Not knowing this is a **pedestrian** precinct, some tourists accidentally drove in this area.　不知道這裡是行人徒步區，有些觀光客不小心在這個區域開車。

18. upgrade [ʌpˋgred] v. 升等；升級

I was very lucky to be the ten thousandth guest of that hotel, and they **upgraded** my single room to an executive room.

我非常幸運成為那間旅館第一萬位旅客，他們把我的單人房升級為高級房。

19. business class [ˋbɪznɪs klæs] n. 商務艙

Seats in **business class** cost much more than seats in economy class.

商務艙的座位價格高於經濟艙。

20. offer [ˋɔfɚ] n. 出價；報價

We'll pay \$6500 for the staff trip. That's our final **offer**.

我們會為這次的員工旅遊付六千五百美元。這是我們最後的報價。

UNIT
5

6 A Complaint Letter

● **Setting:** Purchasing
● **Focus:** Reading Test—Text Completion

I. Warm-up

Goody Electronics Corp. just received a complaint letter from a customer. Let's read the following email and see what problem they need to solve.

✉   − ◻ ✕
To: goodyeleccorp@service.net
From: takizawa0529@treenet.com
Subject: Delayed order and wrong **delivery**
Date: Tue., May 2
Attachment: 📎 **Invoice**

Hello,

My name is Takizawa Masaharu. I'm writing this email in **reference** to the delivery of my order, order #ELE6533. I received it this morning and found that you actually sent me the wrong order.

I **placed an order** for a Blu-ray DVD player (#HD88645) and a stereo (#QR57712) on April 11th. Yet, the order I received contained neither of them, but a toaster and a vacuum cleaner instead. You can check your computer records or the attached electronic invoice, which your ordering system sent after I placed the order.

Moreover, I read on your website that once orders are placed, customers will receive them within ten business days. However, I got the order THREE weeks after placing the order—that is, you **exceeded** the time limit you had promised.

I **assume** you're a responsible company and can well take care of my problem. If someone could please contact me ASAP, I would really appreciate it.

Sincerely,

Masaharu Takizawa

There is a lot of information in the email. Please work with your partner to sort out the information and write A to F in the blanks.

A. What Mr. Takizawa received

B. Order number

C. When Mr. Takizawa placed the order

D. When Mr. Takizawa received the order

E. Product numbers

F. Actions that Mr. Takizawa hopes the company takes

II. Reading

Goody Electronics Corp. has replied to Mr. Takizawa's complaint letter. Let's read the email below and find out how they solved the problem.

UNIT
6

To: takizawa0529@treenet.com

From: goodyeleccorp@service.net

Subject: Re: Delayed order and wrong delivery

Date: Wed., May 3

Dear Mr. Takizawa,

We **apologize** for the late and wrong delivery of your order. We are terribly sorry that we caused you so much trouble and inconvenience.

We used a new ordering and delivery system, and it wasn't working properly. That might have been the cause of the mistake we made. We've made sure that your order was fixed, and we sent it out to you this morning. We'll continue perfecting our ordering and delivery system to avoid similar mistakes in the future.

Please accept our deepest **apology** for the trouble we have caused. We have **enclosed** with your order a 30%-off **coupon** and a $20 gift **certificate**, both of which have no *expiration* date and can be used at any of our stores nationwide. The delivery person will *retrieve* the package that was mistakenly sent when he delivers the correct order.

Sorry again for any inconvenience we caused you.

Sincerely,
Luis Geer
Customer Service Manager
Goody Electronics Corp.

III. Tasks

According to the email, how did Goody Electronic Corp. solve the problem? Tell your classmates and write it below.

_____

_____

IV. Test Tactics

Focus: Reading Test—Text Completion

新制多益的閱讀部份中，段落填空共有四個題組，每題組四題。

題型特色：段落填空題型的選項不只單字和片語，還會出現完整句子。

解題關鍵：掌握句子填空的前後文文意。

以下方試題為例：

Questions 1 to 4 refer to the following job advertisement.

> Job vacancy: -------. They will be in charge ------- assisting the pilots and crew
> **1.** **2.**
> manager to handle various situations in the passenger cabin during a flight.
> Applicants need to have the ability to act quickly in a crisis and show strong ------- to
> **3.**
> changes and situations that might ------- in the middle of a flight. Also, they must
> **4.**
> have their own vehicle to commute to and from the airport, such as a car or
> motorbike.

UNIT
6

1. (A) Levi Airlines is looking to hire two pilots.
   (B) Levi Airlines is looking for two new flight attendants.
   (C) Levi Airlines is hiring two new aircraft mechanics.
   (D) Levi Travel Agency is *looking* for a new travel agent.

2. (A) of
   (B) with
   (C) to
   (D) at

3. (A) adaptation
   (B) adapt
   (C) adaptable
   (D) adaptability

4. (A) arise
   (B) operate
   (C) regard
   (D) search

難度最高的題目為第 1 題句子填空題，解題步驟如下圖：

速讀題目選項內容

題目重點：
要雇用的是 "pilots"、"flight attendants"、"mechanics" 還是 "travel agent"？

判讀填空 前後文

前後文關鍵訊息：
". . . handle various situations in the passenger cabin during a flight."

回答問題

回答問題：
在飛機客艙上處理各種情況是空服員的職務，故選 (B)。

V. Learn by Doing

請完成以下 1–8 題。第 3 題及第 8 題請速讀選項、判讀前後文以迅速解題。

Questions 1 to 4 refer to the following letter.

September 12
Michael Peterson
777 Paradise Rd
Glasgow, G41 2QG, UK

Dear Mr. Peterson,

The china teacups you ordered from Royal Victoria are in this package. *Owing to*

the fact that your purchase exceeded $600, we have ------- to give you a shopping
1.
coupon with great discounts, and a gift certificate that can be exchanged ------- an
2.
exquisite dinnerware set. The coupon and gift certificate are *valid* until September

30. Please use them before they expire. -------. We are truly sorry for the
3.
inconvenience. We ------- its delivery to your home by the end of this week.
4.

Sincerely,

Matthew Johnson
Royal Victoria

1. (A) decide

   (B) decided

   (C) decision

   (D) decisive

2. (A) for

   (B) with

   (C) at

   (D) in

3. (A) There is no need for a receipt
because the items were bought
with a gift coupon.

   (B) You can use the gift coupon at
any of our stores.

   (C) We'd like to make a sincere
apology for not providing you
with an invoice.

   (D) We included the receipt in the
package.

4. (A) certify

   (B) confirm

   (C) guarantee

   (D) examine

 Test tip

新制多益重視測驗考生對文章段落
結構的理解能力。不論是第六部份段
落填空或是第七部份篇章結構題型，
解題的關鍵技巧皆在於前後文的判
讀。

UNIT
6

Questions 5 to 8 refer to the following email.

To: Andrew Jones, Warehouse Manager
From: Jason Bleakley
Date: November 14
Subject: About work ethics in our department

Dear Mr. Jones,

I'd like to ------- an issue about the warehouse. To begin with, I'd like to make -------
    5.   **6.**

to one of the warehouse rules that has recently been *implemented*. The rule states

that workers need to spend at least 15 minutes cleaning out the *aisles* between

storage areas before they finish work. -------, last Monday when I finished work, I
                                                 7.

saw piles of boxes stacked up and blocking the aisles. It seems that some of our

staff haven't *observed* the new rule, so I think punishment for breaking the rule is

now necessary. -------. Thank you.
                8.

Jason Bleakley

5. (A) address
   (B) distribute
   (C) replace
   (D) evaluate

6. (A) refer
   (B) reference
   (C) referring
   (D) referred

7. (A) Otherwise
   (B) However
   (C) Moreover
   (D) In fact

8. (A) Please take my suggestion into consideration.
   (B) Let me explain how to solve this problem.
   (C) I clean up the aisles every day before I go.
   (D) There is no need to punish any member of the staff.

VI. Vocabulary Track-19

1. **delivery** [dɪ`lɪvərɪ] n. 遞送；交貨

Can you accept a time lag between order and **delivery**? We don't offer express shipping now because the New Year holidays are among the busiest delivery days of the whole year.　您能接受訂貨與到貨相隔一段時間嗎?我們目前不提供快遞服務，因為新年假期是全年度配送最繁忙的時刻。

2. **invoice** [`ɪnvɔɪs] n. 發票；出貨單

Lila couldn't find the **invoice** of the TV set she purchased last Friday, thus making it more complicated to process a refund.

Lila 找不到上週五購買電視的發票，因此使得退款的過程更加複雜。

3. **reference** [`rɛfrəns] n. 提及

I am writing this letter in **reference** to your letter of September 7 to respond to the problems of your purchase.　這封信是要回覆您九月七日來函提及的購買問題。

4. **place an order** phr. 下訂單

Customers who **place an order** on our website during the Christmas holidays will get a US$25 gift card.

於聖誕假期期間在我們網站下單購物的消費者將得到一張美金二十五元的禮金卡。

5. **exceed** [ɪk`sid] v. 超過

The total cost of our trip to Europe doesn't **exceed** US$4,000.

我們這趟歐洲之旅的全部花費沒有超過美金四千元。

6. **assume** [ə`sum] v. 以為 ★★★

I **assumed** the handmade soaps produced by Natural Factory would be very expensive, but the prices turned out to be perfectly reasonable.

我本以為 Natural Factory 的手工肥皂一定很貴，結果發現價格竟非常合理。

**UNIT
6**

7. apologize [əˋpɑləˌdʒaɪz] v. 道歉

We **apologize** for any inconvenience we may have caused you.

我們對於任何可能已經造成的不便之處向您致歉。

8. apology [əˋpɑləˌdʒɪ] n. 道歉

David filed a complaint about the quality of B&G Food's products, and he got a written **apology** two days later.

大衛對 B&G Foods 的食品品質提出投訴，兩天後他收到一封書面道歉。

9. enclose [ɪnˋkloz] v. 隨信附上；隨包裹附上

Please **enclose** a copy of the invoice with the returns.

退回商品時請附上發票影本。

10. coupon [ˋkupɑn] n. 優惠券

Judy is a crazy **coupon** collector. She always uses coupons to get groceries at super low prices.

Judy 是個瘋狂的折價券收集者，她總是用折價券取得價格極低的雜貨。

11. gift certificate [ˋgɪft səˋtɪfəkɪt] n. 禮券

The shop gave Hunter a US$30 **gift certificate** as compensation for the inconvenience they caused him.

商店送給 Hunter 美金三十元的優惠券以彌補對他造成的不便。

12. expiration [ˌɛkspəˋreʃən] n. 到期

The **expiration** date of the vouchers is May 28th this year.

現金抵用券的到期日為今年五月二十八日。

13. retrieve [rɪˋtriv] v. 取回；找回

Is it convenient for you to let us **retrieve** the products tomorrow afternoon around three o'clock?　你明天下午三點左右方便讓我們將貨品領回嗎？

14. owing to [`oɪŋ ˌtu] prep. 因為

We purchased office supplies from this store **owing to** its better discounts.

我們因為較好的優惠而向這家店採購辦公室用品。

15. exquisite [ɪkˋskwɪzɪt] adj. 精緻的

Lillian bought the **exquisite** china from one of the finest china shops worldwide.

Lillian 在全世界最好的瓷器商店之一買了這精緻的瓷器。

16. valid [ˋvælɪd] adj. 有效的

The coupon is **valid** between January and March and entitles the holder to 20% off all products in our shop.

優惠券有效期間是從一月至三月，持有者可享全店商品八折優惠。

17. implement [ˋɪmpləmənt] v. 實施；實行

The purpose of **implementing** the new policy is to protect the rights of consumers.

實施新政策的目的在於保障消費者的權益。

UNIT
6

18. aisle [aɪl] n. 通道；(超市貨架間的) 走道

Potato chips and candy are in the second **aisle** from the registers.

洋芋片和糖果在收銀臺數來第二個走道的貨架上。

19. storage [ˋstorɪdʒ] n. 貯藏

The new warehouse will provide enough **storage** space.

新的倉庫將提供足夠的貯藏空間。

20. observe [ˌəbˋzɝv] v. 遵守

All the members of the customer service department should **observe** these rules of etiquette.　所有客服部人員皆須遵守這些禮儀規範。

7 Working Out in a Gym

● **Setting:** Health
● **Focus:** Listening Test—Conversations

I. Warm-up Track-20

Nathan is attending the monthly conference at his company. Their chief executive is **announcing** a new policy. Let's listen to the announcement.

According to the announcement, what benefits is the company going to provide?

☐ a new gym at the company

☐ one hour for using the gym

☐ a free physical examination

☐ free sportswear

☐ free fitness courses

☐ free consulting service offered by a fitness trainer

☐ healthy meals paid partly by the company

II. Reading

After the conference, Nathan goes to ask their health consultant Kaylee Young for some advice. Please pair up and read out their dialogue below.

Nathan: Hi, Ms. Young. I think I'm not fit enough. I haven't exercised for several years. I'd like to get some exercise and become healthier. Can you tell me about the courses you will offer?

Ms. Young: Sure. Our fitness center will have free weightlifting and stretching courses. Which one would you like?

Nathan: Stretching sounds great.

Ms. Young: Good choice! It is important to choose what you'll enjoy.

Nathan: That's true! I used to do activities that I found boring or too difficult. I think that's why I failed to stick with them. In addition to taking the stretching course, what else do you suggest I do?

Ms. Young: You can start walking on a treadmill for 20 minutes a day.

Nathan: Walking for 20 minutes only? Why not one hour?

Ms. Young: You'd better set a realistic goal. Don't push yourself too hard. After you walk 20 minutes a day for two weeks, you can move up to half an hour.

Nathan: That makes sense. When do you recommend me exercising, in the morning, afternoon or evening?

Ms. Young: It depends. Exercise when you are energetic.

Nathan: I see. I'll exercise in the morning, 'cause I'm a morning person.

Ms. Young: Good. Making exercise a habit isn't too easy. Remember, be patient and never give up.

Nathan: I will! I know I may meet some setbacks, but I'll keep on working out anyway.

Ms. Young: That's the spirit. I also recommend you find a workout partner. You can encourage and motivate each other.

Nathan: That would be a nice idea. Thanks!

Ms. Young: By the way, if you really want to be fit, exercising isn't all you need to do. You should also get enough sleep, keep a **balanced diet**, and drink at least 2000 cc of water per day.

Nathan: OK, I'll keep your words in mind. Thank you so much.

UNIT
7

III. Tasks

Nathan is now taking notes of what Ms. Young told him. Let's help him write down the health tips Ms. Young mentioned.

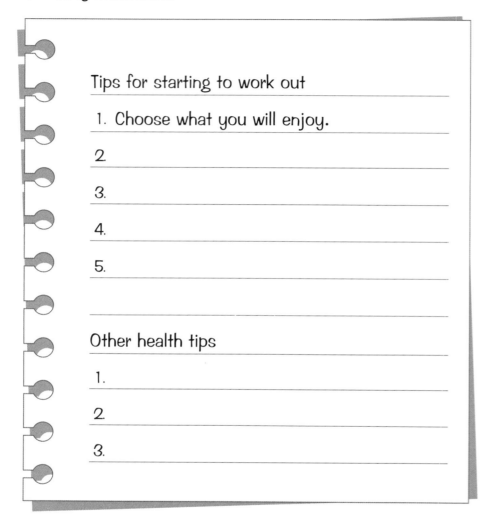

Tips for starting to work out

1. Choose what you will enjoy.

2.

3.

4.

5.

Other health tips

1.

2.

3.

IV. Test Tactics

Focus: Listening Test—Conversations

新制多益中聽力部份的對話題共有 13 個題組。

題型特色： 1.會測驗閱讀圖表及整合資訊的能力。

2.會測驗對於說話背景及話語隱含意思的理解能力。

解題關鍵： 1.對話播放前先速讀題目，對話播放時專注聽取關鍵資訊。若題目結合圖表，

則聽力結束後需整合圖表資訊後作答。

2.速讀題目時若看到 Why does the man / woman say, "..."? 的問題，則聽力

播放時須特別注意聆聽那句話的說話背景並理解其前後文文意。

以下方試題為例：

例題一　Track-21

Item	Original Price
Vitamin B	$6.50
Vitamin C	$7.50
Calcium	$9.00
Massage machine	$100.00

Look at the graphic. What is the price of the massage machine today?

(A) $70.00　　　　(B) $80.00　　　　(C) $90.00　　　　(D) $100.00

UNIT
7

解題步驟：

1　速讀題目，掌握題目關鍵字 "price of the massage machine"

2　聽取關鍵訊息 "I'm also interested in buying a massage machine . . . They are 20% off now."

3　搭配圖表訊息，按摩器原價 $100.00，打八折後為 $80.00，得答案為 (B)

例題二 Why does the man say, "That's a pity"? Track 22

(A) He knows the phone can't be repaired.

(B) He feels sorry that the service wasn't satisfying.

(C) He doesn't know who the rude man is.

(D) He feels sorry that the phone was broken.

解題步驟：

 1 速讀題目，掌握題目關鍵句 "That's a pity"

 2 聽取前後文，得知 "That's a pity" 是男子回應女子對服務的抱怨

3 得答案為 (B) He feels sorry that the service wasn't satisfying.

V. Learn by Doing   Track-23

請完成以下 1–9 題。請利用對話與對話間的間隔時間預先速讀題目，以掌握關鍵資訊。

BODY WEIGHT (lb)	DOSAGE (tsp)
below 85	3/4
86–135	1
136–185	1 and 1/4
over 186	1 and 1/2

1. Where most likely are the speakers?

   (A) At a gym

   (B) At a pharmacy

   (C) At a laboratory

   (D) At a supermarket

2. What does the man recommend?

   (A) Vitamin supplements

   (B) Laboratory equipment

   (C) Nutritious food

   (D) Cold medicine

3. Look at the graphic. How much does the woman weigh?

   (A) Below 85 pounds

   (B) Between 86 and 135 pounds

   (C) Between 136 and 185 pounds

   (D) Over 186 pounds

4. What does the man want to get repaired?

   (A) A dumbbell

   (B) An exercise bike

   (C) A treadmill

   (D) A television

5. Why does the woman say, "we need to sort out the situation first"?

   (A) She wants to know which part is broken.

   (B) She wants to tell how much the repair will cost.

   (C) She wants to know if the man broke the item.

   (D) She wants to know if the item is within warranty.

6. What does the woman ask the man to do?

   (A) Give contact details

   (B) Come back in three days

   (C) Fix the item

   (D) Pay a maintenance fee

UNIT
7

7. What is the conversation mainly about?

    (A) A job application

    (B) A complaint about service

    (C) The impact of a policy

    (D) A method of removing information

8. Which department does Mr. Watson most likely work in?

    (A) Customer service

    (B) Risk management

    (C) Human resources

    (D) Information technology

9. Why does Mr. Watson say, "No problem"?

    (A) He is happy to accept Sandra's application.

    (B) He thinks he just did his duty.

    (C) He feels it is easy to make the decision.

    (D) He doesn't mind Sandra giving the short notice.

 Test tip

新制多益的對話更加模擬真實的英語對話情境。對話內容轉折不多，但來回交談頻繁；會出現口語中常見的省略音 (elision，如 going to→gonna)；且會出現三人對話題型。

VI. Vocabulary Track-24

1. **announce** [əˋnaʊns] v. 宣布

The boss **announced** that every employee will have a free medical checkup this year.　老闆宣布今年每個員工都將有免費的健康檢查。

2. **introduce** [ˌɪntrəˋdjus] v. 推行；開始實施

The human resources department is **introducing** new employee benefits policies.
人力資源部將推行新的員工福利政策。

3. **under construction** phr. 建造中

The community gym is still **under construction**. Residents of that neighborhood are looking forward to its opening.
社區運動中心仍在興建中，附近居民很期待它開幕。

4. **estimate** [ˋɛstəˌmet] v. 估計

The cost of building the gym is **estimated** at 20 million dollars.
建造體育館的費用估計為兩千萬元。

5. **instructor** [ɪnˋstrʌktɚ] n. 教練

The fitness **instructor** patiently explained how to use the exercise equipment.
健身教練耐心說明運動器材的使用方式。

6. **aim** [em] n. 目標

Olivia exercises daily with the **aim** of losing ten pounds in two months' time.
Olivia 每天運動是為了在兩個月內減輕十磅。

7. **efficiency** [ɪˋfɪʃənsɪ] n. 效率；效能

Taking regular breaks can help you achieve better work **efficiency**.
定時的休息能幫助你達到較好的工作效率。

UNIT
7

8. subsidize [ˋsʌbsəˌdaɪz] v. 給予補貼；資助　★★★

The employee fitness program is heavily **subsidized**.

員工的健身課程得到大量補貼。

9. balanced diet [ˋbælənst ˋdaɪət] n. 均衡的飲食　★★★

A **balanced diet** offers our bodies nutrients of all kinds.

均衡的飲食提供我們的身體各種養分。

10. tablet [ˋtæblɪt] n. 藥片，錠　★★★

Grace takes one vitamin **tablet** every morning.

Grace 每天早上都吃一錠維他命。

11. relieve [rɪˋliv] v. 減輕，減緩　★★★

David took medicine to **relieve** his stomachache.

David 吃藥以減輕他的胃痛。

12. chronic [ˋkrɑnɪk] adj. 慢性的，長期的　★★★

Adam has suffered from **chronic** back pain since his sixties.

Adam 從六十幾歲開始就有長期的背痛。

13. oblige [əˋblaɪdʒ] v. 使有義務；強制　★★★

A company is **obliged** to pay their employees' salaries.

公司有義務支付員工薪水。

14. malfunction [ˌmælˋfʌŋkʃən] v. 運轉失常，故障　★★★

The treadmill has **malfunctioned**, but you can use the exercise bike instead.

跑步機故障了，但你可以使用這臺運動腳踏車。

15. fever [ˋfivɚ] n. 發燒　★★★

This medicine can help reduce your **fever** and ease your headache.

這個藥物能幫助你退燒並減緩頭痛。

16. **sore throat** [ˌsor ˋθrot] n. 喉嚨痛

I'm starting to have a **sore throat** and a stuffy nose. I think I've got a cold.

我開始喉嚨痛且鼻塞，我覺得我是感冒了。

17. **remedy** [ˋrɛmədɪ] n. 藥物；療法

The physician says the **remedy** can fight off flu.

醫生說此藥物能夠對抗流感。

18. **infection** [ɪnˋfɛkʃən] n. 感染；傳染病

You'd better see a doctor about the **infection** in your right eye.

你最好找醫生看看你右眼的感染。

19. **symptom** [ˋsɪmptəm] n. 症狀

You need to describe the **symptoms** to your doctor, so that he can diagnose your illness.

你需要向醫生描述症狀，這樣他才能診斷你的病情。

20. **pharmacy** [ˋfɑrməsɪ] n. 藥房，藥局

Elena bought a bottle of cough syrup from a **pharmacy**.

Elena 從藥局買了一瓶咳嗽糖漿。

UNIT
7

8 Hiring the Right Employees

I. Warm-up

Matthew took over as an HR (human resources) assistant recently. He is now searching on the Internet for articles about recruitment. Let's read one article he just found.

Sophia Jones

Former Vice-president of HR of BestTech and a well-known blogger

Tips for Hiring the Right Employees

Competent and energetic employees will lead a company to success, while hiring the wrong employees is costly and *time-consuming*. I hope the following tips will help you find the right ones.

1. Write a clear job description before hiring an employee.
   The candidates may not be clear about the *responsibilities*, necessary *qualifications*, and possible salary of a particular job by just looking at the job title. It is therefore recommended that a detailed job description be written to *clarify* what the job involves.

2. Review résumés, applications, and *credentials* carefully.
   In your recruiting process, there should be a list of the key characteristics that a well-*qualified* candidate must possess. Keep the list in mind while reviewing the résumés, applications, or credentials. In that way, you can *weed out* candidates *unsuitable* or less qualified for the job.

3. Take the soft skills into consideration.
   Although professional skills may seem the first and most *essential criteria* for choosing the right employee, soft skills are something you should also take into consideration. Social intelligence, interpersonal skills, *communication* skills, and emotional intelligence are very important in teamwork.

Hope you found this article helpful, and good luck with your recruiting!

Below are some qualities that candidates may have. Which are soft skills? Which can be the proof of professional skills? Fill out the table with the letters and discuss your answers with your partner.

A. able to solve problems independently

B. patient with colleagues

C. competent to carry our every task

D. always punctual

E. willing to listen to others

F. with certifications

G. with a **bachelor's degree**

H. willing to work in groups

Proof of professional skills	Soft skills

II. Reading

The recruiting manager Ms. Evans gives Matthew a job application letter she just received. Let's read it together with Matthew.

Scarlett Sky

156 Mount State Road, Georgetown, CA 98067

Home: 0141 294 5698   Cell: 07551 56977

E-mail: scarlettsky412@tmail.com   **1**

October 14

Peyton Evans

Recruiting Manager

LookFurther Design Corp.

58 Delaware Road

Hatfield, CA 98065

Dear Ms. Evans,

I am writing to apply for the administrative assistant position you are **advertising** for on the website helpfindjobs.com. As requested, I am enclosing my résumé, the job application, my certification in general administrative assisting, and two references.

UNIT

8

After reading the job description, I am certain I would be a perfect fit for the position. I am an experienced and efficient office administrator. I previously worked as an administrative assistant for over four years. I am proficient with office software suites and good at filing, faxing, entering data, answering multiple phone lines and emails, and so forth. I am also confident about my ability to handle multiple tasks and learn new skills.

I am not afraid to ask questions, and I possess good listening and communication skills. My former colleagues liked me for always being easy-going and willing to help. Whenever issues arise, I always act as a problem solver, not a bystander.

I would welcome the opportunity to meet with you to further discuss my qualifications for working for LookFurther Design Corp. I really believe I am a *competitive* candidate for this position and hope I will be considered. Please give me a chance to be a great *addition* to your company. Thank you for your consideration. I look forward to hearing from you.

Yours sincerely,

Scarlett Sky

III. Tasks

A. There is a lot of information in the letter. Please work with your partner to sort out the information and write A to E in the blanks.

    A. the applicant's contact details

    B. the applicant's characteristics

    C. the applicant's professional skills

    D. the applicant's expectations

    E. the applicant's work experience

B. If you were Matthew, would you invite Scarlett for an interview? Why or why not? Tell your classmates.

IV. Test Tactics

Focus: Reading Test—Triple Passage Reading

新制多益中閱讀部份的三篇閱讀測驗共有三個題組，每題組五題。

題型特色：測驗閱讀理解速度及資訊整合能力。

解題關鍵：採用 SSG 多篇閱讀測驗解題步驟 (Summarize the texts. → Skim the questions. → Gather the information.) 作答。

以下方試題為例：

Questions 1–5 refer to the following notice, email, and book review.

Green Hill Publishing Company is hiring a senior editor to join the fiction section to help produce novels. As the senior editor in the fiction section, you will be responsible for identifying promising authors in the field, developing book projects, and editing **manuscripts**. Candidates should have at least two years of fiction editing experience and stay in tune with the fiction book market. Excellent editing and writing skills are required. The ideal candidate is also expected to display creativity and good logical thinking skills. Please send a **cover letter** and a CV to Lillian Wilson at hrdepartment@greenhill.com by the end of this month.

To: hrdepartment@greenhill.com.

From: sarahsarah@cmail.com

Date: January 25

Subject: Job application

Attached: Sarah Abbot's CV

Dear Ms. Wilson,

I am interested in the senior editor's position at your company. I have three years of fiction editing experience. I have developed a novel series *The Zombie World*, which can be proof of my keen eye for the book market and my ability in finding great authors and producing best-selling books. I believe my ability qualifies me for consideration. If you give me this opportunity, I will definitely help you produce novels that cater to the **mass market**.

I have attached my CV, and I look forward to discussing my qualifications with you. Thank you for your consideration.

Sincerely,

Sarah Abbot

UNIT
8

> *The Zombie World*
>
> *The Zombie World* is not a typical zombie story. Written by Gabriel Cooper, it is a novel series that combines global disaster, social criticism and humor that keeps the pages turning. Unlike most zombie stories, this one actually makes you think about the things that are going on around you. It makes critical **commentary** of many **phenomena** around the world and weaves it into the plot. *The Zombie World* is a book series you should not miss!
>
> Rating: Must read

1. What is suggested about Green Hill Publishing Company?

    (A) It is hiring an assistant editor.

    (B) It publishes works of fiction.

    (C) It is interested in zombie stories.

    (D) It has published a popular novel series.

2. When was the notice most likely posted?

    (A) In January

    (B) In February

    (C) In March

    (D) In April

3. Why does Sarah mention *The Zombie World* in her letter?

    (A) To show that she is competent

    (B) To promote the book series she developed

    (C) To express her interest in sci-fi movies

    (D) To depict the phenomena around the world

4. What does Sarah look forward to?

    (A) Being promoted

    (B) Selling more novels

    (C) Going for an interview

    (D) Writing book reviews

5. What is most likely true about Gabriel Cooper?

    (A) He criticizes social phenomenon seriously.

    (B) He is a best-selling author.

    (C) He writes typical zombie stories.

    (D) He cooperates with Green Hill Publishing Company.

解題步驟如下：

Summarize the texts. 摘要文章主旨

1. 公告：Green Hill Publishing Company 正招募小說組資深編輯一名
2. email：Sarah 應徵當編輯，表示曾製作小說系列 *The Zombie World*
3. 書評：*The Zombie World* 由 Gabriel Cooper 所著，是與眾不同的喪屍故事

Skim the questions and gather the information.
速讀問題並搜集資訊

Q1. Green Hill 的資訊：從公告 "fiction section" 得答案為 (B)
Q2. 公告的時間：根據公告，求職者必須在本月月底前寄出求職信，而根據 email 寄信日期可推知公告最有可能是在一月公佈，得答案為 (A)
Q3. 提到 *The Zombie World* 的原因：根據 email，該小說可作為 Sarah 的實力證明，得答案為 (A)
Q4. Sarah 的期待：根據 email，Sarah 信末表示期待面談，得答案為 (C)
Q5. Gabriel Cooper 的資訊：從書評知其為 *The Zombie World* 的作者，再從 email 得知 *The Zombie World* 能證明 Sarah 挖掘好作者並製作出暢銷書的實力，推知答案為 (B)

Test tip

> 多益單篇及雙篇閱讀可採用典型的 SSA 解題步驟 (Skim the questions. → Scan the text. → Answer the questions.)，但多益三篇閱讀不建議從題目出發，反而應採用從閱讀文章出發的 SSG 解題步驟，以更快速地整合資訊並避免誤入題目陷阱。

UNIT
8

請完成以下 1–5 題，練習使用 SSG 多篇閱讀測驗解題技巧。

Questions 1–5 refer to the following notice, article and letter.

Hometown Books

Dear Beloved Readers,

It is with great regret that Hometown Books will close on August 31 after being here for more than five decades. As the only local bookstore in Wood Town, we have been so pleased to have served our community all of these decades. During the month before we close, we will have activities to thank those who have supported us and to celebrate our history and shared love of reading.

Wood Town Is Changing

With the opening of the new shopping mall at the north end of town, many of our beloved local businesses have been lost. We have witnessed the loss of Al's Pizza and Rosa's Bakery. And now our old bookstore meets the same fate. They will close after their Summer Reading Season this year. It seems that all the good old things in our town are going to be gone.

We know Mayor Clarke values the economic benefits of the new shopping mall and its ability to bring in business from neighboring towns. However, does she feel how the soul of our community is being lost? Some things can't be brought back. Our community soul will never be the same again.

Dear Editor,

I like your article about the changes in Wood Town. I have spent many Saturday afternoons walking the sidewalks of our lovely town. I would enjoy a pizza, browse through books at the old bookstore, and top it off with a cream pie. However, things have changed. The soul of our community is being lost.

I know we can't stop the march of change. Nevertheless, some things are worth preserving. It would be nice if our mayor could find a way to preserve the history of our town while growing our local economy at the same time.

Natalie Thomas

1. What is the most likely reason why Hometown Books is closing?

   (A) The owner is too old.

   (B) Business is being drawn away by a mall.

   (C) Books are too expensive nowadays.

   (D) People would rather watch a movie than read a book.

2. What will Hometown Books most likely do during this year's Summer Reading Season?

   (A) Celebrate their history

   (B) Found a reading club

   (C) Renovate their bookstore

   (D) Order newly published books

3. Why did Natalie write to the editor?

   (A) To propose a project

   (B) To apply for a job

   (C) To comment on an article

   (D) To suggest writing more articles on this topic

4. Which business was probably the last one Natalie visited on Saturday afternoons?

   (A) Hometown Books

   (B) Al's Pizza

   (C) The new mall

   (D) Rosa's Bakery

UNIT
8

5. What is Ms. Clarke advised to do?

   (A) Open a new bookstore

   (B) Close the shopping mall

   (C) Preserve the local history

   (D) Stop growing the local economy

VI. Vocabulary   Track-25

1. **time-consuming** [ˋtaɪmkənˋsumɪŋ] adj. 耗時的

   Finding the right employees can be very **time-consuming** if there is no strategy or direction.　如果毫無策略和方向，尋找合適的員工是很費時的事。

2. **responsibility** [rɪˌspɑnsəˋbɪlətɪ] n 職責

   The assistant's **responsibilities** include filing and entering data.

   助理的職責包括文件歸檔和輸入數據資料。

3. **qualification** [kwɑlɪfɪˋkeʃn] n. 資格，必備條件

   Technology skills and a high level of proficiency in English are necessary **qualifications** for this job.　運用科技的技能與高水平的英文是這份工作的必備條件。

4. **clarify** [ˋklærəˌfaɪ] v. 釐清；闡明

   The chief executive officer was requested to **clarify** his stand on the issue.

   執行長被要求澄清他在該問題上的立場。

5. **credential** [krɪˋdɛnʃəl] n. 資格證明

   New employees are required to submit copies of their academic **credentials**.

   新員工被要求繳交學歷證明影本。

6. **qualified** [ˋkwɑləˌfaɪd] adj. 有資格的，符合條件的

   After finishing the training program, you will be **qualified** for this job.

   完成此訓練課程後，你將符合這項工作的條件。

7. **weed out** phr. 剔除，淘汰

   Two thirds of the candidates will be **weeded out** at the first interview.

   三分之二的求職者會在第一場面試中被剔除。

8. unsuitable [ʌn`sutəbl̩] adj. 不適合的

The HR department will screen out **unsuitable** candidates according to their test results. 人力資源部將根據測驗結果淘汰不適合的求職者。

9. essential [ə`senʃəl] adj. 必要的；基本的

We value punctuality as an **essential** characteristic of an employee.

我們視守時為員工的必要特質。

10. criterion [kraɪ`tɪrɪən] n. 衡量標準 複 criteria

The main **criterion** for increasing an employee' salary is the employee's overall job performance. 員工加薪的主要衡量標準是看員工的整體工作表現。

11. communication [kə,mjunə`keʃən] n. 交流；溝通

Excellent **communication** and interpersonal skills are Susan's valuable assets.

極佳的溝通技巧和人際關係技巧是 Susan 具有的重要優勢。

12. bachelor's degree [`bætʃələ˞s dɪgri] n. 學士學位

Our new secretary is a graduate of Washington University with a **bachelor's degree** in marketing. 我們的新祕書畢業於華盛頓大學，擁有行銷學的學士學位。

13. advertise [`ædvɚ,taɪz] v. 打廣告 (推銷、徵聘)

We're going to **advertise** for two persons to assist in this project.

我們打算刊登廣告應徵兩個人協助這個企劃。

UNIT
8

14. competitive [kəm`pɛtətɪv] adj. 有競爭力的；競爭的

To our surprise, the youngest job applicant is the most **competitive** candidate for that position. 讓我們驚訝的是，最年輕的應徵者是那個職位最有競爭力的候選人。

15. addition [ə`dɪʃən] n. 增加物；附加物

The new assistant will be a great **addition** to our group.

新增聘的助理會對我們這個組別非常有幫助。

16. manuscript [`mænjə,skrɪpt] n. 原稿，未出版的稿件 ★★★

The writer has sent the novel **manuscript** to a publisher.

作家已將小說原稿寄給一家出版社。

---

17. cover letter [`kʌvə lɛtə] n. 附信；寄履歷時附加的求職信 ★★★

Please include a **cover letter** when you mail out your résumé.

寄履歷時請附上求職信函。

---

18. mass market [,mæs `markɪt] n. 大眾市場 ★★★

The new releases are expected to do very well in the **mass market**.

新發行的產品被預期能在大眾市場上表現亮眼。

---

19. commentary [`kamən,tɛrɪ] n. 評論 ★★★

Ian wrote his social and political **commentaries** in this new book.

Ian 在這本新書中寫下他對於社會及政治的評論。

---

20. phenomenon [fə`namənən] n. 現象　複 phenomena ★★★

Mass layoffs were a **phenomenon** of the recession.

大規模裁員是經濟衰退時期的現象。

旅遊英文這樣就GO

包辦你旅行時會用的英文,有了這一本旅遊說英文再也不用怕。
羅列出境、入境、住宿等大大小小旅行中可能會碰到的情境。

許惠姍　審訂
三民英語編輯小組　彙編

「字彙出外景」認識該課情境會用到的英文字彙,讓你出國不必再大眼瞪小眼。

「旅遊狀況句」模擬旅遊期間會遇到的狀況,讓你應對得宜、對答自如。

「還能這樣說」列舉其他可能的對答句子,讓你輕鬆應對各種突發狀況。

「現在才知道」帶你認識各地風俗及旅遊小祕訣,退散旅行會遇到的煩心事。

10堂課練就TED Talks演講力

溫宥基　編著
車昀庭　審定

掌握TED Talks 演講祕訣，
上臺演講不再是一件難事。

★ **為你精心挑選的演講主題**
全書共10個主題，別出心裁的主題設計，帶出不同的學習重點，並聘請專業的外籍作者編寫每一課主題的文章，讓你輕鬆融入TED Talks 演講主題。

★ **為你探討多元的關鍵議題**
涵蓋豐富多元的議題教育融入課程，包括生命、資訊、人權、環境、科技、海洋、品德、性別平等之多項重要議題，讓你多方面涉獵不同領域題材。

★ **為你培養敏銳的英文聽力**
每堂課的課文和單字皆由專業的外籍錄音員錄製，提升你的英文聽力真功夫。

★ **為你增強必備的實用單字**
每篇課文從所搭配的TED Talks 演講影片精選出多個實用單字，強化你的單字庫。

★ **為你條列重要的演講技巧**
搭配精采的10個TED Talks 演講影片，傳授最實用的演講技巧，並精準呈現演講的常用句型。

★ **為你設計即時的實戰演練**
現學現做練習題，以循序漸進、由淺入深的教學引導，將每一堂課所有的演講技巧串聯並整合即完成一場英文演講，練就完美的演講力。

Let's TOEIC

可搭配108課綱加深加廣選修課程

根據多益
最新改制題型

NEW TOEIC
新多益

黃金互動16週：進階篇 二版
解析本

🎧 附電子朗讀音檔、解析本、模擬試題

李海碩、張秀帆、多益900團隊 編著
Joseph E. Schier 審定

★ 每回以多益測驗常見情境設計，符合新多益命題趨勢。
★ 量身打造任務型導向課堂活動，培養解決問題的能力。
★ 隨書附贈一回200題模擬試題，提升你英文聽讀能力。

三民書局

Unit 1

I. Warm-up

1. factory　　2. Friday　　3. 0809; 3341

聽力腳本

Good afternoon, Ms. Harvey. This is Joanna Jacobs from Cape Steel Company. Earlier this week, we scheduled a meeting for Wednesday at 9:00. I'm very afraid we need to reschedule the meeting because my boss, Mr. Lynch, was sent to **inspect** the factory in Illinois **at short notice**. I'm terribly sorry. Mr. Lynch will be back this Thursday night. He can meet your boss any time on Friday. Please give me a call and let me know when would be convenient for you. Do you have my number? I think you do, but in case you don't, my number is 234–0809, extension 3341. Sorry again for the **inconvenience**. If Friday isn't convenient for you, just call me and we'll see how to work it out. Talk to you soon. Bye-bye.

午安，Havey 女士。我是 Cape Steel 公司的 Joanna Jacobs。本週稍早，我們排定週三上午九點開會。恐怕我們需要重新安排會議時間，因為我的老闆 Lynch 先生，臨時被通知要去伊利諾州的工廠視察。我非常抱歉。Lynch 先生週四晚上回來。他可以在週五任何時間和您的老闆見面。請打電話給我，讓我知道你們什麼時間方便。您有我的電話號碼嗎？我想您有，但萬一沒有，我的電話號碼是 234–0809，轉分機 3341。很抱歉造成您的不便。如果週五你們不行就打電話給我，我們來看看如何解決。不久再談。再見。

II. Reading

Dawson：你好，Wasada 先生。可以跟你聊聊嗎？

Wasada：好呀。什麼事？

Dawson：我聽說，我們與目前的印表機供應商合約即將到期，所以我提議換成和 Power Print 合作。印表機服務供應商要能提供穩定的品質和例行的維修，但現在這家沒做到。

Wasada：我注意到了你過去兩週已對於印表機的問題提出十次申訴。

Dawson：是的。當我終於完工，檔案卻印不出來，真的很讓人火大。而且我相信這些干擾會對員工的生產力造成負面影響。我們應該要求和收費的高低相應的服務品質。

Wasada：我了解。到目前為止，你遭遇過哪些印表機的問題呢？

Dawson：墨水匣不是高容量的，因此我必須定期填充。因為不熟悉，我有時會不小心把油墨灑出來，搞得一團糟。

Wasada：我知道印表機的油墨很難洗掉，幾乎沒辦法從衣物上去除。

Dawson：確實如此。我經常弄髒我的裙子。更別提卡紙、列印品質不良及油墨堵塞。雖然 Power Print 是一家兩年前才成立、相當新的印表機供應商，但在辦公室設備領域廣受推薦。所以我強烈建議您考慮此項提議。

Wasada：我理解你感受到的不便。然而 Power Print 比起我們現在的供應商貴一些。我必須將此事呈報給營運長 Casey 先生。他是做最終決定的人。

Dawson：我懂。關於這件事，我該去和他聯絡嗎？

Wasada：我覺得我來向他提出此建議也許比較合適。

Dawson：好的。非常謝謝你。祝你有美好的一天，Wasada 先生。

Wasada：你也是。

III. Tasks

Mr. Casey, I just met Ms. Dawson, and she told me that there are some problems with the printers in the office. The problems include the cartridges' extremely limited capacity, paper jams, poor print quality, and ink clogging. So she suggests that we change to another provider, Power Print. This provider is a bit expensive, but widely recommended and indeed more reliable. (答案僅供參考)

IV. Test Tactics

| 1. A | 2. B | 3. B | 4. B | 5. B | 6. B | 7. A | 8. B |

V. Learn by Doing

| A. | 1. A | 2. B | 3. C | 4. D | 5. D | 6. C |
| B. | 7. D | 8. C | 9. A | 10. B | | |

A.

聽力腳本

1. (A) The kids are playing chess.
   (B) The kids are eating cheese.
   (C) The kids are boarding a bus.
   (D) The kid is chasing his friend.
   (A) 孩子在下棋。
   (B) 孩子在吃起司。
   (C) 孩子正在上公車。
   (D) 孩子在追他的朋友。

2. (A) There is a cross on the little boy's shirt.
   (B) The family is crossing the road.
   (C) There are zebras on the roadside.
   (D) The family is constructing the road.
   (A) 小男孩的襯衫上有十字架。
   (B) 那家人正在過馬路。
   (C) 路邊有斑馬。
   (D) 那家人正在築路。

3. (A) The rain is pouring in the forest.
   (B) The friends are reading books.
   (C) The woman is pouring a drink.
   (D) The waiter is serving food.
   (A) 森林裡下起傾盆大雨。
   (B) 朋友們正在看書。
   (C) 女子正在倒飲料。
   (D) 服務生正在上菜。

4. (A) She is lending a book.
   (B) She is putting a book on the shelf.
   (C) She is passing a book to her friend.
   (D) She is examining a book.
   (A) 她正出借一本書。
   (B) 她正把書放上書架。
   (C) 她正把書拿給她的朋友。
   (D) 她正在檢視一本書。

5. (A) The vending machines are all empty.
   (B) The bending machines are functioning in the factory.
   (C) Venders are standing in front of the machine.
   (D) Snacks and drinks are available in the vending machines.
   (A) 販賣機全都是空的。
   (B) 折彎機在工廠裡作業。
   (C) 小販站在機器前面。
   (D) 販賣機裡能買到零食和飲料。

6. (A) The goods are lined on the ground.
   (B) Customers are shopping indoors.
   (C) The man is checking something on the car.
   (D) The merchandise is being packed.

(A) 貨品排列在地上。

(B) 顧客在室內採購。

(C) 男子正在看車上的東西。

(D) 商品正被打包裝箱。

B.

7. 如果經理使用有效的溝通策略，員工可以更有效率地工作。

    (A) 工作 (現在式)　　　　(B) 可以工作 (現在式)　　(C) 工作 (過去式)　　　　(D) 可以工作 (過去式)

8. 如果公司取得足夠的資金的話，這個計畫將已經完成了。

    (A) 取得 (現在式)　　　　(B) 取得 (過去式)　　　　(C) 取得 (過去完成式)　　(D) 取得 (現在完成式)

9. 如果 Graysen 完成這項具挑戰性的任務，他的主管會將他派去總部。

    (A) 完成 (第三人稱單數)　(B) 完成 (原形動詞)　　(C) 完成 (過去式)　　　　(D) 完成 (未來式)

10. Owen 公司可能已經達成更高的銷售量，如果他們早一個月推出產品的話。

    (A) 可能達成 (過去式)　　　　　　　　　　　(B) 可能已經達成 (過去完成式)

    (C) 可能達成 (現在式)　　　　　　　　　　　(D) 可能已經達成 (現在完成式)

Unit 2

I. Warm-up

cash international checks; deposit it; 12; two; one

政策修訂通知

    我們對如何執行銀行業務，做了一些調整。請遵循以下新政策：

- 客戶想存款入戶，必須是該帳戶的所有人或授權代理人。
- 客戶想存入或提取現金，必須出示至少一項政府核發的身分證明文件。
- 客戶想兌現或存入支票，必須出示至少兩項政府核發的身分證明文件。
- 客戶出示支票之前，必須先在支票背面簽名。
- 我們不允許兌現國際支票。客戶必須先將國際支票存入戶頭，最少十二天後才可提款。

    規定即日起在我們所有分行生效。這些調整協助我們打擊洗錢等犯罪行為。

    謹慎處理現金和支票。讓我們把 C&B 變成大家能信賴的銀行。

II. Reading

致目前與未來的客戶們：

我們很高興宣布 C&B 銀行已經和 WestWorld 銀行達成最終協議，我們將併購 WestWorld 銀行及其在全美各地的兩百四十六家分行。

WestWorld 銀行是華盛頓地區第二大獨立銀行，總資產值估計近十五億美元，存款額估計十一億美元。合併一定能讓兩家銀行的市場自然擴增。

併購之後，一百萬名 WestWorld 銀行的客戶，加上各分行目前聘雇的大約四千五百名員工，都將移轉至 C&B 銀行。這是一個強而有力的合夥關係，植基於 WestWorld 銀行的卓越名聲，以及 C&B 銀

行的完善資源。聯手後，C&B 銀行網絡將擁有五百八十八家分行，並成為美國四大銀行之一。

我們將始終堅持信念——致力將客戶擺在第一位。我們的首要任務永遠都會是維持強大的客服聲譽，C&B 過去二十七年正是因為此聲譽而和其他銀行有所區別。

讓我們一起展望更光明燦爛、前程遠大的未來。

C&B 銀行執行長
Kerry T. White 敬上

III. Tasks
☐ the total assets of C&B Bank
☑ the total assets of WestWorld Bank
☑ the branch number of C&B Bank after the combination
☑ the branch number of WestWorld Bank
☐ the number of staff members of C&B Bank
☑ the number of staff members of WestWorld Bank
☐ the four largest banks in the U.S.
☑ the first piority of C&B Bank
☑ how many years C&B Bank has been serving customers (答案僅供參考)

V. Learn by Doing
1. C　2. A　3. C　4. B

Valleyhill 青少年俱樂部
Buford 公路 65 號
Doraville 市，GA 30340

十二月十五日
Enrique Bascunana
Doraville 市政府社區發展部部長

親愛的 Bascunana 先生：

Valleyhill 青少年俱樂部非常感謝您個人和 Doraville 市給我們的的支持。我們的方案讓許多孩童在放學後和週末有個地方可去，要不然可能無處可去。[1] 我們的社區非常多元，小孩聚在一起參加有趣的活動，也是件好事。

我們現在有很多孩童，正遭遇空間不足和其他資源的問題。[2] 在我們的俱樂部和河流之間有一大塊市政府所有的未利用土地。要是我們能取得那塊地，我們將能進一步擴展方案，興建足球場，這是很多孩子們會喜歡的。[3]

如果政府能允許我們利用那塊地建足球場，那會是我們的最佳選項。[4] 我們將能容納更多孩童，給他們一個放學後能活動的安全環境。

我們要再度感謝社區發展部門，長期支持我們在此地的作為，同時希望他們可以協助我們，進一步服務社區孩童。

Valleyhill 青少年俱樂部

青少年活動主任　劉約瑟敬上

1. 劉先生為什麼寫信給 Bascunana 先生？
   (A) 為 Valleyhill 青少年俱樂部爭取更多錢
   (B) 討論他們計畫中形形色色的學生
   (C) 要求使用 Doraville 市擁有的土地
   (D) 取得核可在他的土地上蓋足球場
2. 關於 Doraville，文中提到了什麼？
   (A) 有許多不同種族背景的孩童。
   (B) 孩童放學後立刻回家。
   (C) Doraville 市不在乎那些孩童。
   (D) 那些孩童全是白人，而且講英語。
3. 下句最適合放在文中標示 [1], [2], [3], [4] 的哪一處？
   「然而，我們沒有財務資源可買下這樣一大片土地。」
   (A) [1]　　　(B) [2]　　　(C) [3]　　　(D) [4]
4. 如果 Valleyhill 青少年俱樂部獲得許可，他們最可能做什麼？
   (A) 投資房地產　　(B) 蓋足球場　　(C) 擴充辦公室　　(D) 買塊土地

Unit 3

I. Warm-up

1. luxurious vacation　2. battery; touch; tablet　3. 2 points; 1 point　4. 40%　5. returned

聽力腳本

Attention, all my dear salespeople! It's our time to shine and set a new record! Our annual sale is coming, which as usual also means we're gonna have a sales contest! This year, the prize is a luxurious vacation for two in Tahiti!

The annual sale is from August 15th to August 25th! Seize every chance to sell our products! Before the contest begins, I want to remind you what products you should promote. It's close to back-to-school week, so we can expect that many college students, especially freshmen, will come to BestMart. If they do not have special *technological* requirements, you should recommend the new *line* of laptops manufactured by David Tech. Besides the long-*lasting* battery and long-term *durability*, the laptops are featherweights and have touch capability and a foldable keyboard. That is, they are *capable* of *functioning* either as a laptop or a *tablet*.

If you sell one David Tech laptop, you get two points. Moreover, domestic appliances sold will get you one contest point each. However, if the merchandise purchased during the annual sale is returned, the points will be *deducted* from your contest records. Tell customers that they can get discounts of up to 40%. They will be sorry if they leave BestMart with empty hands! Go set a record! Good luck!

所有親愛的銷售員，請注意。這是我們發光發熱和刷新紀錄的時刻！我們的年度特賣馬上到了，這也一如往常表示我們會有銷售比賽！今年，獎品是大溪地豪華雙人假期！

　　年度特賣從 8 月 15 日到 8 月 25 日！要抓緊每一個機會銷售我們的產品！比賽開始前，我想提醒你們哪些是需要促銷的商品。馬上就到開學季了，我們可以預期會有很多大學生來 BestMart，特別是大一新鮮人。如果他們沒有特定科技上的需求，你們應該推薦 David 科技公司生產的新款筆電系列。此系列筆電除了電池壽命長又經久耐用外，重量極輕且有觸控功能及可折疊的鍵盤。也就是說，它們能當成筆電用，也可當成平板用。

　　如果你賣出一臺 David 科技的筆電，可獲得兩點。此外，每賣一臺家電，可獲得一點。然而，如果在年度特賣期間賣出的商品被退貨，點數會從你的比賽紀錄裡扣除。請告訴顧客他們能獲得最低六折的折扣優惠。如果他們空手離開 BestMart 一定會後悔！去創紀錄吧！祝好運！

II. Reading

　　我以前對 Feather 電腦的評價很高，但在買下一臺 Feather 4322 型號的 15 吋筆電後我就改觀了。我八月二日在 BestMart 買下這臺筆電，這只是四個月前的事。這表示我的電腦還在一年有限保固期內。我打了好幾次客服專線，但他們不是讓我在線上等，就是把我轉接到各個不同部門。到最後，一位諮詢人員告訴我這是軟體問題。他連一眼都沒看我的電腦，怎能確認這是軟體問題？

　　我的電腦不斷發出嘈雜噪音，而且常常無故關機。此外，無線網路經常無法連線。如果很幸運沒有斷網，我的電腦就會變得超級慢。下載一個網頁平均費時五分鐘。所以基本上，這臺電腦現在已經是個沒用的金屬盒子。在我的案例裡，我沒看到 Feather 電腦支援它的產品或保固服務。我非常失望。

　　我將送出一份電腦問題報告到客服電郵信箱。我要求你們解決這些問題，而非將問題丟回給我。請儘快與我聯絡。我的手機號碼是 0912–123–123。希望你們能努力挽回顧客的心。

III. Tasks

2. August 2nd

3. (3) 4322　　☐12"　　☐13"　　☐14"　　☑15"　　☐17"

4. ☐ 1. Can't connect a printer to the computer

　　☐ 2. Blue Screen of Death

　　☑ 3. The computer is too slow.

　　☑ 4. The computer shuts down on its own.

　　☑ 5. Can't connect to the Internet

　　☑ 6. The computer makes noises.

　　☐ 7. The computer can't recognize a USB device.

　　☐ 8. The computer hardware doesn't work properly.

　　☐ 9. Any other. Please specify: _____

6. 0912–123–123

IV. Test Tactics

聽力腳本

And now for our weekly news Bulletin Board. Charlie Johnson will be holding a concert in the National Auditorium on the fifth of March this year. This event will be incredible because this will be the first time Charlie Johnson sings together with another superstar, Stella Walker. The tickets for children are not on sale. The discounted adult tickets have been sold out. All the money raised from this concert will be donated to fighting lung cancer and promoting a healthy, smoke-free lifestyle. Get in while you have a chance to buy a ticket and enjoy this special event.

V. Learn by Doing

| 1. A | 2. D | 3. B | 4. D | 5. C | 6. A | 7. C | 8. D | 9. B | 10. A | 11. A | 12. B |

聽力腳本

Questions 1 through 3 refer to the following announcement and list.

Hello, Isaiah Electronics shoppers. I regret to inform you that we are planning to close down June 20th, so starting from the 1st of June, we are having a clearance sale. A full list of the ***bargains*** we will be offering is available in the ***pamphlet*** at the front door. Please don't forget to get one on your way out. Please note that keyboards will have 5% more discount than listed. This is a chance to grab some nice high quality bargains, so don't miss out. We will be opening a new electronics store called IsaiahTech in Sunnybank Shopping Center as of July 1st. Please don't forget to come and give us a visit.

請參考以下的聲明和列表回答第 1 題至 3 題。

您好，Isaiah 電器的購物者。很遺憾通知您，我們計畫六月二十日關門歇業，所以自六月一日起開始清倉大拍賣。放在前門的小冊子裡有關於我們會提供的優惠的完整清單。請不要忘記離開時拿一份。請注意鍵盤折扣會比表列的多 5%。這是撿些好康的機會，所以別錯過。我們七月一日會在 Sunnybank 購物中心開一家新的電器店，叫做 IsaiahTech。請別忘記來我們的店看看。

品項	折扣
穿戴式科技產品	40%
耳機	50%
鍵盤	37%
滑鼠	50%
硬碟	12%

1. 為什麼店內有特賣？
   (A) 他們要關門歇業。　　　　　　　　　(B) 他們正為盛大開幕進行宣傳。
   (C) 他們正要推出新產品。　　　　　　　(D) 他們正在慶祝週年慶。

2. 請看圖表。鍵盤的折扣為何？
   (A) 32%　　　　　(B) 37%　　　　　(C) 40%　　　　　(D) 42%

3. 顧客在何處可以看到折扣的清單？
   (A) 官網　　　　　(B) 前門　　　　　(C) 地方報紙　　　　　(D) 櫃臺

Questions 4 through 6 refer to the following announcement and menu.

Attention, passengers! Welcome aboard Lewis Train. We are heading for Brisbane City and will arrive in approximately five hours time. At this time, please make sure that your carry-on bags are not blocking the aisle, but are placed under your seat or in the baggage compartment above your head. As our trip is rather long, we do offer passengers beverages and simple meals on the way to our destination. Please refer to the menu in the train brochure in your seat-back pockets. The menu describes the pricing for each food and drink item. To promote vegetarian food, all vegetarian choices will have an extra one dollar off. Train staff will begin to sell the food and drink in 30 minutes from now.

請參考以下的廣播和菜單回答第 4 題至 6 題。

各位乘客請注意！歡迎搭乘 Lewis 火車。我們正前往布里斯本，大約五小時後抵達。現在請確定您的隨身行李沒有擋住走道，而是放在您的座位下或是您頭頂的行李櫃。由於旅途漫長，我們在抵達目的地的路上會提供乘客飲料和簡餐。請參考椅背後置物袋內的火車手冊裡的菜單。菜單裡有每種食物和飲料品項的價錢。為推廣素食，所有的蔬食選項都將再享額外一元的折扣。火車服務人員三十分鐘後將開始販售食物和飲料。

食物／飲料	價格
可樂	$5.50
礦泉水	$4.50
素食便當	$7.00
水果沙拉	$8.35

4. 火車往哪裡開？
   (A) 雪梨　　　　　　(B) 墨爾本　　　　　　(C) 圖翁巴　　　　　　(D) 布里斯本
5. 請看圖表。今天素食便當要多少錢？
   (A) $4.50　　　　　　(B) $8.35　　　　　　(C) $6.00　　　　　　(D) $7.00
6. 廣播說火車服務人員稍後會做什麼？
   (A) 供應食物和飲料　　(B) 進行緊急狀況演習　(C) 查票　　　　(D) 發表公告

Questions 7 through 9 refer to the following excerpt from a meeting and chart.

Attention everyone. Let's get down to business. We have finished calculating and evaluating our annual sales totals. Here is a chart that summarizes the sales we made from cell phones over each **quarter** during the last business year. As you can see, we hit a high of $46,000,000 during the first quarter. However, due to the influence of competitors, our sales dropped to $40,000,000 in the second quarter. Fortunately, during the third quarter, the sales rose to $44,000,000, and during the fourth quarter, the sales reached a new peak, thanks to our new marketing projects. For the first quarter of next year, we are hoping to increase our sales revenue by another 10%.

請參考以下的會議談話節錄和圖表回答第 7 題至 9 題。

大家請注意。我們來談正事。我們已計算且評估完我們的年度銷售總額。這裡是一張圖表，摘錄我們上年度每季銷售手機的銷售額。如你們所見，我們在第一季達到四千六百萬元的高峰。然而，受競爭者的影響，我們的銷售額在第二季降到四千萬元。所幸銷售額在第三季上揚至四千四百萬元，並且在第四季，拜我們新行銷方案所賜，銷售額達到新高峰。我們希望明年第一季的銷售收入可再增加 10%。

7. 說話者最可能在何種公司工作？
   (A) 房地產公司　　　(B) 家具公司　　　　(C) 手機公司　　　　(D) 硬體公司
8. 請看圖表。公司因新的行銷方案獲得的銷售額為多少？
   (A) 四千六百萬元　　(B) 四千萬元　　　　(C) 四千四百萬元　　(D) 四千七百萬元
9. 公司對於下一季有什麼希望？
   (A) 銷售額成長 15%　(B) 銷售額成長 10%　(C) 廣告收益成長 15%　(D) 廣告收益成長 10%

Questions 10 through 12 refer to the following speech and graphic.

On behalf of Wintek International, I would like to thank you for your awarding us the Gold Stevie Award. Our CEO John Davidson started our company in 1998 for the purpose of advocating environmental protection and the use of natural materials to construct modern cars. We rebuild used cars and then sell them on the market for a profit. Thus, we are able to recycle waste material and reuse it for a useful, profitable purpose, making the world a cleaner and less polluted place. Owing to the fact that global warming is becoming a serious problem, our company has started to create fuels that are derived from natural substances which don't greatly increase the level of CO_2 emissions.

請參考以下的發言和圖表回答第 10 題至 12 題。

我想代表 Wintek 國際公司，感謝您頒給我們 Stevie 金獎。我們的執行長 John Davidson 在 1998 年創立公司，目的是提倡環境保護，並使用天然材料打造現代汽車。我們重製二手車，然後在市場上出售獲利。所以，我們能夠為了實用和獲利的目的回收廢棄材料，讓世界變成更乾淨、汙染更少的地方。由於全球暖化逐漸成為一個嚴重的問題，我們公司已經開始開發由天然材料製成、不會大幅增加二氧化碳排放量的燃料。

獎項名稱	頒獎對象
Stevie 金獎	環境友善企業
Stevie 銀獎	高獲利企業
企業大獎	高成長企業
Stevie 銅獎	成功新創事業

10. 請看圖表。Wintek 的屬於哪種類別的企業？
   (A) 環境友善企業　　　　(B) 高獲利企業　　　　(C) 高成長企業　　　　(D) 成功新創事業

11. 執行長創辦公司的主要目的為何？
   (A) 保護環境　　　　　　　　　　(B) 賺大錢
   (C) 與其他汽車公司競爭　　　　　(D) 開發來自天然材料的燃料

12. 公司為何開發新燃料？
   (A) 獲取巨大利潤　　(B) 減少全球暖化　　(C) 吸引消費者　　(D) 更瞭解環境汙染

Unit 4

I. Warm-up

！這封電子郵件以高重要性傳送
寄件人：nelsoncole@hdlightcorp.net
收件人：gillianjones@hdlightcorp.net
主旨：商展前應完成事項
日期：11 月 8 日　星期一
Gillian 你好： 我們即將前往參加維吉尼亞州商展。這是本公司一項重大活動，希望透過這次商展，我們會獲得較多

訂單和合約。以下是我需要你做的事——準備一份關於我們所有的 LED 照明產品的簡短報告，並在報告當中置入我們現有客戶的名單。請最晚於星期四中午前將這份報告傳給我。也請在十一月二十日之前完成下列兩項任務：

(1) 和設計部門見面討論我們傳單的全新版面設計。請在送交印刷廠前先寄給我新的設計圖以進行最終審核。

(2) 替總經理和行銷總監訂兩盒名片。他們是我們公司的商展代表。

如果你需要協助，請讓我知道。如果有必要，我會指派助理給你。我知道你一直很勤奮可靠。請再接再厲！

行銷經理
Nelson Cole

II. Reading

給青年創業家和行銷主管的工作坊		
12 月 1 日週三	Vast 會議中心	上午 9:00 至下午 4:00
上午 9:00– 上午 10:00一和企業家講師群相見歡！		
上午 10:00– 中午 12:00一工作坊　時段一 第一會議室：提高生產力的六步驟 (Strongwill 商業專家主講) —— 想拓展你的公司嗎？你需要更多產品！如果你希望生意興旺起來，絕對不能錯過這場演講！ 第二會議室：如何開始我的事業 (HighQ 商業顧問公司主講) —— 想成為自己的老闆嗎？想成為成功的創業者嗎？對於預備資金和選擇開業地點，想要有更多瞭解嗎？來找我們吧！ 第三會議室：如何在網路上賺錢 (成功青年網路創業家 Jack Johnson 主講) —— 想成為網路事業營運大咖嗎？這位二十歲的年輕人將與你分享他的成功經驗。如果錯過這個絕佳機會，你會後悔！		
中午 12:00– 下午 2:00一午餐		
下午 2:00– 下午 4:00一工作坊　時段二 第一會議室：當網路行銷天才，一年進帳六位數 (NetKing 主講) —— 你不會相信在網路上賺錢可以有多麼簡單。給你自己一個機會去了解所有訣竅，成為網路之王。 第二會議室：如何找到絕佳產品來賣 (Elizabeth Jr. Wu 主講) —— 你該批發買進什麼產品？這個產品會熱銷嗎？採購是門學問！ 第三會議室：行銷人員必須精通的四項祕訣 (Janet Jane 主講) —— 精通良好交易的有效策略並掌握市場風向！來給自己一點激勵並學習更多有關行銷的事！		
工作坊門票在報到處可取得。 下午 4:00 至 6:00 可用門票在 Penny's 酒吧換取免費飲料。		

V. Learn by Doing

1. B	2. D	3. D	4. C	5. B

Somerville 學區

北達科他州 Somerville 市

工作職缺

中學社會研究課老師：誠徵六至八年級社會研究課教師。必須有州政府發出的教師證以及至少五年教學經驗。

資訊科技助理：誠徵當地小學的資訊科技助理。需有相關領域的學士學位。必須精通多種軟體程式，處理硬體的基本技能也不可或缺。主要職責是在軟體使用上協助教師。

辦公室助理：Central 高中的英文部辦公室需要一名助理。需有學士學位。職責包括支援教師及為部門辦公室提供行政支援。曾在學校工作為佳，但並非必要條件。

請將履歷及求職信寄至：May Alcott, hiring@somervilleschools.edu

收件人：hiring@somervilleschools.edu

寄件人：rodrigo425@yakoo.com

日期：5 月 21 日

主旨：中學社會研究課教師職

附件：RodrigoLacasa.doc; 證書 .pdf; 推薦信一 .pdf; 推薦信二 .pdf

親愛的 Alcott 女士：

您好。我的名字是 Rodrigo Lacasa。我寫信是想詢問有關於中學社會研究課教師的職位。我有南達科他州教授六至十二年級社會研究課的教師證，而我現在想搬到北達科他州。我已執教超過十年，包括在菲律賓美國學校教了兩年。

我知道我仍然必須取得北達科他州的教師證，我預計今年年底能拿到。我已附上我的履歷、南達科他州教師證的掃瞄影本以及兩封推薦信。

我一直熱愛教授社會研究。我相信歷史和社會科學扮演了重要的角色，能夠影響學生如何看待這個世界和看待自己。如果你能給我這個機會，我會十分感激。

Rodrigo Lacasa 敬上

---

1. 此網頁的對象是誰？

(A) 學區的職員　　　　　　　　　　　　(B) 在學區找工作的人

(C) 在菲律賓的美國學校工作的人　　　　(D) 新聞媒體

2. 關於 Lacasa 先生，下列何者為真？

(A) 他沒有寄求職信。　　　　　　　　　(B) 他沒有任何教師證。

(C) 他已經教書超過十二年。　　　　　　(D) 他尚未完全符合他申請的工作的資格。

3. Lacasa 先生覺得他還需要多久時間才會取得北達科他州教師證？

(A) 大約一個月　　(B) 大約三個月　　(C) 大約五個月　　(D) 大約七個月

4. 如果你有基本的電腦技巧並剛從大學的社會系畢業，你符合哪一個工作的資格？

(A) 中學社會研究課老師 (B) 資訊科技助理　　　(C) 辦公室助理　　　(D) 以上皆是

5. 電子郵件中，第三段第二行 pivotal 一字最接近的字義是

(A) 類似的　　　　　(B) 重要的　　　　　(C) 著名的　　　　　(D) 典型的

Unit 5

I. Warm-up

Noah needs to pay $ ___398___ .

聽力腳本

Front desk: Phoenix Hotel, how may I help you?

Noah: Hi, I'd like to make a reservation for the second Friday in July, July 13th.

Front desk: Sure. May I have your name, please?

Noah: Noah Williams.

Front desk: Mr. Williams, how many people is the reservation for?

Noah: Two, so I would like a twin room. Do you still have any *vacancies*?

Front desk: Please hold on while I check that for you. Oh, I'm sorry, sir. The only rooms we have available on July 13th are on the executive floor. Would you like a deluxe room or an executive room? They're *spacious* and comfortable.

Noah: How much does a deluxe room cost?

Front desk: It's $148 a night.

Noah: That's acceptable. Do you have a twin room available the next two days, July 14th and 15th?

Front desk: Yes.

Noah: That's good! I'll book a deluxe room for July 13th, and a twin room for the 14th and 15th.

Front desk: OK. Your rooms are reserved. Could you give us your phone number?

Noah: It's 0987–520–377. If I need to make any *adjustment* to my reservation, I'll call you *in advance*.

Front desk: Sure. Goodbye, Mr. Williams. Thanks for calling.

前臺：這裡是 Phoenix 飯店，請問需要什麼協助？

Noah：您好，我想訂房間，七月的第二個星期五，七月十三日。

前臺：沒問題。請問您的大名？

Noah：Noah Williams。

前臺：Williams 先生，您訂的房間是要給幾個人住呢？

Noah：兩個人，所以我想要雙床雙人房。你們還有空房嗎？

前臺：我幫您查一下，請不要掛電話。噢，很抱歉，先生。七月十三日剩下的房間都在行政樓層。您想要豪華客房還是行政客房？這些房間寬敞又舒適。

Noah：豪華客房要多少錢？

前臺：一晚是一百四十八美元。

Noah：可以接受。接下來兩天，七月十四和十五日，還有雙床雙人房嗎？

前臺：有的。

Noah：很好！我七月十三日訂一間豪華客房，十四日和十五日訂一間雙床雙人房。

前臺：好。您的房間已經訂好了。您可以留下您的電話號碼嗎？

Noah：0987-520-377。如果我需要調整預約，會先打電話給你。

前臺：好的。再見，Williams 先生。謝謝您的來電。

II. Reading

Wyatt：嘿，Noah。你現在有空討論行程嗎？

Noah：好呀。我正考慮第一天去拉斐那。

Wyatt：真巧！拉斐那剛好是我想參觀的首選！

Noah：哇！太棒了！那裡有很多餐館，專賣炸海鮮——炸鯊魚佐大蒜醬、酥炸小魚和炸魷魚。

Wyatt：聽起來好美味！我們剛好都愛吃海鮮。太完美啦！

Noah：而且我發現最受歡迎的餐廳是 Agoni Grammi。我們可以在那裡吃午餐再喝幾杯清涼的啤酒。

Wyatt：然後我們下午可以在碼頭旁放鬆，看漁船進進出出。我們也可以在附近長長的海灘散步。

Noah：好極了！然後我們可以叫飯店接駁車載我們回去，我們的第一天就可以在飯店提供的吃到飽自助晚餐中畫下句點。

Wyatt：至於第二天，我想參觀在蘇尼恩的波塞頓神廟。那屬於希臘很棒的文化遺產。

Noah：好主意。我知道在古代，雅典水手把那座廟視為他們出海駛離雅典時最後看到的文明象徵，以及回程時最早看到的文明象徵。

Wyatt：哇，真有趣！那地方似乎有許多故事。你知道詩人拜倫將他的名字刻在神廟的大理石柱上嗎？

Noah：真的？真是個有趣的軼事！也許是某個頑皮的觀光客刻上去的。反正，我們可以去找那個刻字然後在那裡拍張照。

Wyatt：然後我們可以去斯尼斯，那是個漂亮的海灘。

Noah：我的旅遊書上說那個海灘有個松樹林，而且那裡的水通常很乾淨。

Wyatt：最重要的是，那裡的水很溫暖。我們可以在那游泳。但海邊也可能有很多人，因為七月是旺季。

Noah：沒關係。我們可以找到地方游泳。

Wyatt：噢！我們先這樣吧。我現在必須回去工作了。

Noah：好的。晚點聊。

III. Tasks

Rafina;

Relax by the harbor, watch fishing boats, stroll along the beach;

shuttle;

Sounion;

Visit the temple of Poseidon;

swim

IV. Test Tactics

2. A

Possible indirect responses: I'd like to visit that place again.

I liked the people there.

It's a shame you couldn't join us.

You should go there once in your life!

3. A

Possible indirect responses: The Wi-Fi password is 1212.

I'm afraid it isn't working now.

You will need an account first.

Sorry, it's only for staff. (答案僅供參考)

聽力腳本

1. Are there any vacancies at your hotel?

   (A) I am afraid you need to try the one across the road.

   (B) We are looking for a new hotel vice-manager.

   (C) The hotel has a very spacious lobby.

2. How did you like the trip?

   (A) I was in love with the culture.

   (B) I went to Greece.

   (C) I like to go on trips.

3. Could we have **access** to the Wi-Fi?

   (A) The login information is on the table.

   (B) Yes, you're welcome to swim in the back.

   (C) Just make yourself at home.

V. Learn by Doing

1. B	2. B	3. A	4. A	5. A	6. B	7. C	8. C

聽力腳本

1. I'm calling to confirm the **cancellation** of my flight to LA.

   (A) Would you like an aisle seat or a window seat?

   (B) May I have your ticket number please?

   (C) Here is your luggage tag.

   我打電話來確認是否已取消我飛往洛杉磯的班機。

   (A) 你想要靠走道還是窗戶的位子？

   (B) 可以告訴我你的機票號碼嗎？

   (C) 這是你的行李牌。

2. How is the service in the hotel?

   (A) The view is great.

   (B) Can't find anything better around.

   (C) There are two job openings.

   旅館的服務如何？

   (A) 視野很棒。

   (B) 附近找不到更好的了。

   (C) 有兩個職缺。

3. Is there complimentary breakfast?

   (A) Served from seven every morning.

   (B) Free Wi-Fi.

   (C) Room for two, please.

   有附贈早餐嗎？

   (A) 每天早上七點開始供應。

   (B) 免費 Wi-Fi。

   (C) 我要雙人房。

4. Where is the **pedestrian** crossing around here?

   (A) The footbridge is over there.

   (B) Look both ways before crossing.

   (C) They are walking around.

   附近的行人穿越道在哪裡？

   (A) 天橋就在那裡。

   (B) 過馬路前左右都要看。

   (C) 他們在附近逛逛。

5. Can I refund my ticket?

   (A) Sorry, only within one day of purchase.

   (B) Round-trip, please.

   (C) The funding is sufficient.

我可以退票嗎？

(A) 退款，僅購票一天內可以。

(B) 我要來回票。

(C) 資金很充裕。

6. Could I *upgrade* to *business class*?

(A) The business is good.

(B) I am afraid it's full.

(C) The class is over.

我可以升級到商務艙嗎？

(A) 生意很好。

(B) 恐怕已經客滿。

(C) 課程已經結束。

7. Don't you think the *offer* is bad?

(A) I will offer him a bed.

(B) Yes, the prices are really good.

(C) Let's try to bargain.

你不覺得這個出價很差嗎？

(A) 我會給他一張床。

(B) 是的，價格真的很好。

(C) 我們來討價還價吧。

8. Is delivery of luggage included in the price?

(A) The price is good.

(B) At all costs.

(C) Only for frequent customers.

這個價錢包含運送行李嗎？

(A) 價錢不錯。

(B) 不惜一切代價。

(C) 僅限定於常客。

Unit 6

I. Warm-up

1. B	2. E	3. C	4. A	5. D	6. F

| 收件人：goodyeleccorp@service.net |
| 寄件人：takizawa0529@treenet.com |
| 主旨：訂單延遲且出貨錯誤 |
| 日期：5 月 2 日星期二 |
| 附件：發票 |

您好：

我的名字是 Takizawa Masaharu。我寫這封電子郵件是要說有關於我的訂單送貨問題，訂單編號是 ELE6533。我今早收到貨，發現你們其實送錯了。

我在四月十一日下單購買藍光 DVD 播放機 (#HD88645) 和音響 (#QR57712)。然而，我收到的貨沒有上述任何一件，反而是烤麵包機和吸塵器。你可以查你的電腦紀錄或是附件的電子發票。電子發票是你們的訂購系統在我下單後傳送過來的。

此外，我在你們的網站上看到，顧客會在下單後十個工作日內收到貨。然而，我下單後三週才收到貨——也就是，你們超過了你們承諾的時限。

我認為你們是一家負責任的公司，會好好處理我的問題。如果有人能儘快聯絡我，我會不勝感激。

Takizawa Masaharu 敬上

II. Reading

收件人：takizawa0529@treenet.com
寄件人：goodyeleccorp@service.net
主旨：回覆：訂單延遲且出貨錯誤
日期：5 月 3 日星期三
親愛的 Takizawa 先生： 我們為您的訂單出貨延遲且出錯致歉。我們非常抱歉造成您這麼多的麻煩和不便。 我們之前使用新的訂購和出貨系統，而運作並不順利。那可能是我們出錯的原因。我們已確定解決了您的訂單問題，並在今天早上將您訂購的商品寄出。我們將持續改善我們的訂購和出貨系統，避免未來再出現類似的錯誤。 對於我們所造成的困擾，我們致上最深的歉意，請您接受。我們已經隨貨附上一張七折優惠券和一張二十元禮券，兩者都沒有到期日，並且可以在我們全國任一家分店使用。送貨員送貨到府時會取回之前送錯的包裹。 造成您的不便，我們再次致歉。 Goody 電子公司 客戶服務經理 Luis Geer 敬上

III. Tasks

They apologized for their late and wrong delivery and sent the customer the right order, a 30%-off coupon, and a $20 gift certificate. (答案僅供參考)

IV. Test Tactics

1. B   2. A   3. D   4. A

V. Learn by Doing

1. B   2. A   3. C   4. C   5. A   6. B   7. B   8. A

請參考以下的信件回答第 1 題至 4 題。

9 月 12 日 Michael Peterson 天堂路 777 號 英國格拉斯哥 郵遞區號 G41 2QG 親愛的 Peterson 先生： 您從 Royal Victoria 訂購的瓷杯在這個包裹裡。由於您的購物超過六百元，我們決定給您一張大折扣

的優惠券以及一張可以換到一組精美餐具的禮券。優惠券和禮券的有效期限為九月三十日。請在失效前使用。沒提供您發票，我們誠摯道歉。我們真的很抱歉造成您這樣的不便。我們保證週末前送至您府上。

Royal Victoria 公司
Matthew Johnson 敬上

1. (A) 決定 (原形動詞)   (B) 決定 (過去分詞)   (C) 決定 (名詞)   (D) 果斷的
2. (A) 取得   (B) 和   (C) 在   (D) 在…裡面
3. (A) 毋須收據，因為商品是用禮券買的。   (B) 你可在任何一家分店使用這張禮券。
    (C) 沒提供您發票，我們誠摯道歉。   (D) 我們將收據附在包裹裡。
4. (A) 證明   (B) 確認   (C) 保證   (D) 檢視

請參考以下的電子郵件回答第 5 題至 8 題。

收件人：倉儲經理 Andrew Jones
寄件人：Jason Bleakley
日期：11 月 14 日
主旨：關於部門的工作倫理

親愛的 Jones 先生：

我想要說關於倉庫的一件事。首先，我想提及倉庫最近實施的一項規定。這項規定要員工在結束工作之前，必須花至少十五分鐘打掃儲貨區域之間的走道。然而，上週一當我結束工作時，我看到一堆堆的箱子疊在一起，擋住了走道。似乎我們還有部分員工沒遵守新規定，所以我認為違規的處分現在有其必要性。請考慮我的建議。謝謝。

Jason Bleakley

5. (A) 談論   (B) 分配   (C) 取代   (D) 評估
6. (A) 提及 (原形動詞)   (B) 提及 (名詞)   (C) 提及 (現在分詞)   (D) 提及 (過去分詞)
7. (A) 否則   (B) 然而   (C) 此外   (D) 事實上
8. (A) 請考慮我的建議。   (B) 讓我解釋如何處理此問題。
    (C) 我每天下班前打掃走道。   (D) 沒必要處罰任何一位員工。

Unit 7

I. Warm-up

☐ a new gym in the company
☐ one hour for using the gym
☐ a free physical examination
☐ free sportswear

☑ free fitness courses
☑ free consulting service offered by a fitness trainer
☑ healthy meals paid partly by the company

聽力腳本

I'm happily announcing that we're gonna *introduce* a free exercise program for all our employees. There will be an employee gym right on the third floor. It's currently *under construction* and is *estimated* to open in two weeks from now. You'll have one hour a day to use the gym. You can also take free fitness courses and get free advice on how to exercise from Kaylee Young, our health consultant and fitness *instructor*. Our *aim* is to help you reduce your work stress and everyday stress, and we hope to boost your work performance and *efficiency*. Besides, to improve your health, we will also offer *subsidized* meals that are nutrient-rich. Remember, you are our most valuable assets! After all, happy employees make a company flourish.

我很高興宣布我們將推出免費的運動方案給所有員工。員工健身房就設在三樓。目前正在施工中，預計兩週後開放。你們每天可使用健身房一小時，也可以上免費健身課程，並獲得健康顧問和健身教練 Kaylee Young 有關如何運動的免費諮詢。我們的目的是幫助你們減輕工作壓力和日常壓力，也希望提高你們的工作表現和效率。此外，為了促進你們的健康，我們也提供有補貼的營養豐富的餐點。請記住，你們是我們最寶貴的資產！畢竟，快樂的員工才能讓公司蓬勃發展。

II. Reading

Nathan: 你好，Young 女士。我覺得我的身體不夠強健。我好幾年沒運動。我想運動一下，變得更健康。你能跟我說說你們所提供的課程嗎？

Ms. Young: 當然可以。我們的健身中心會有免費的舉重和伸展課程。你喜歡哪一種？

Nathan: 伸展聽起來不錯。

Ms. Young: 好選擇！選擇你會喜歡的很重要。

Nathan: 真的！我以前做過我覺得很無聊或太困難的運動。我想這就是為什麼我無法堅持下來的原因。除了上伸展課程之外，你還建議我做什麼？

Ms. Young: 你可以開始每天在跑步機上走二十分鐘。

Nathan: 只走二十分鐘嗎？為什麼不走一小時？

Ms. Young: 你最好設定一個實際的目標。別對自己太嚴苛。在你每天走二十分鐘達兩週之後，可以增加至半小時。

Nathan: 有道理。你建議我什麼時候運動呢，早上、下午還是晚上？

Ms. Young: 這不一定。在你精神好的時候運動。

Nathan: 我懂了。我要早上運動，因為我這人早上最有精神。

Ms. Young: 很好。養成運動習慣並不容易。記住，要有恆心，絕不放棄。

Nathan: 我會的，我知道我可能會遇到一些挫折，但無論如何我會持續運動。

Ms. Young: 這種精神就對了。我也建議你找個運動夥伴。你們可以彼此鼓勵打氣。

Nathan: 那會是個好主意。謝謝！

Ms. Young: 對了，如果你真的想要很健康，光是運動是不夠的。你還應該有充足的睡眠，保持均衡飲食，並且每天至少喝兩千毫升的水。

Nathan: 好的，我會記住你的話。非常謝謝你。

III. Tasks

Tips for starting to work out

2. Set a realistic goal.
3. Exercise when you are energetic.

4. Be patient and never give up.

5. Find a workout partner.

Other health tips

1. Get enough sleep.

2. Keep a balanced diet.

3. Drink at least 2000 cc of water per day.

IV. Test Tactics

聽力腳本

例題一

M: Hi, have you been here before?

W: No, I'm new to your shop. I need you to help me find some items.

M: No problem. What are you hoping to buy?

W: I'm looking for vitamin C and calcium supplements. Which aisle are they in?

M: Aisle seven. Vitamin **tablets** are on sale, and we're offering a buy four get one free deal on the calcium supplements.

W: OK, thanks. I'm also interested in buying a massage machine to **relieve** my **chronic** back pain. Where is it located?

M: Aisle three. Our massagers have a heating function, so they can soothe your muscles. They are 20% off now.

Question: Look at the graphic. What is the price of the massage machine today?

例題二

W: Hello, I'm Ms. Brown. I'm calling to talk about the poor quality of the service your branch store offers.

M: Hello Ms. Brown, I'm sorry to hear that. Could you please tell me the details of what happened?

W: The cell phone I bought from your store stopped working last week. I called your branch to ask how to get a refund, but the man who answered the phone was very rude. He kept saying that they were not **obliged** to give me a refund.

M: That's a pity. It seems that the man didn't inform you we actually offer repair service if your phone **malfunctions** within the warranty period. Could you tell me which branch store you called and when you called them?

Question: Why does the man say, "That's a pity"?

V. Learn by Doing

| 1. B | 2. D | 3. A | 4. C | 5. C | 6. A | 7. A | 8. C | 9. D |

聽力腳本

Questions 1 through 3 refer to the following conversation and graphic.

M: Hello, can I help you?

W: I've got a cold. I have a **fever** and a **sore throat**. I'd like to buy some over-the counter medicine.

M: OK. I recommend this brand of medicine. It's an effective **remedy** for colds and other **infections**. It should be able to relieve your **symptoms**.

W: That's good. Could you tell me how often I should take it and how much I should take?

M: It says on the directions that you should take it every four hours. As for how much you should take, you need to look at the dosage chart by yourself.

W: Oh, I see it. I'd need to take three quarters of teaspoon.

請參考以下的對話和圖表回答第 1 題至 3 題。

男：您好，需要我幫忙嗎？

女：我感冒了。我發燒還有喉嚨痛。我想買一些成藥。

男：好的。我推薦這個牌子的藥。這能有效治療感冒和其他感染疾病。應該能夠緩解你的症狀。

女：很好。能告訴我應該多久服用一次，以及該服用多少嗎？

男：使用說明上寫著，你應該每四小時服用一次。至於該服多少，你需要自行參照用量表。

女：哦，我看到了。我必須服用四分之三匙。

體重 (磅)	用量 (茶匙)
85 以下	3/4
86–135	1
136–185	1 又 1/4
186 以上	1 又 1/2

1. 說話者最有可能在哪裡？
   (A) 健身房　　　　　(B) 藥房　　　　　(C) 實驗室　　　　　(D) 超市

2. 男子推薦了什麼？
   (A) 維他命保健食品　　(B) 實驗室設備　　(C) 營養的食物　　(D) 感冒藥

3. 請看圖表。女子有多重？
   (A) 不足 85 磅　　　　　　　　　　(B) 介於 86 至 135 磅間
   (C) 介於 136 至 185 磅間　　　　　(D) 超過 186 磅

Questions 4 through 6 refer to the following conversation.

M: Hello, the treadmill I bought at your store has been playing up. I'd like to get it repaired.

W: Sure, sir. When did you buy the treadmill? Is it still within the warranty?

M: Well, it was bought about 14 months ago and the warranty lasts for three years. I can get it fixed free of charge, right?

W: Yes, but we need to sort out the situation first. You must tell us whether the treadmill started to malfunction by itself or whether you did anything to damage it.

M: It played up by itself.

W: OK, could you please leave us your name and contact details? The treadmill will be ready within three weeks or so.

請參考以下的對話回答第 4 題至 6 題。

男：你好，我在你們店裡買的跑步機故障了。我想送修。

女：好的，先生。您這臺跑步機是什麼時候買的？還在保固期內嗎？

男：嗯，大約十四個月前買的，保固期是三年。可以免費維修對不對？

女：是的，但是我們必須先釐清狀況。您必須告訴我們，這臺跑步機是自行發生故障，還是您做了任何事導致它損壞。

男：它自己壞的。

女：好的，您可以留下名字和聯絡資訊嗎？跑步機大約會在三週內修好。

4. 男子想要修什麼？

(A) 啞鈴 　　　　　　　 (B) 健身腳踏車 　　　　　 (C) 跑步機 　　　　　　 (D) 電視機

5. 女子為什麼說「我們必須先釐清狀況」？

(A) 她想知道是哪個零件壞了。 　　　　　　 (B) 她要評估維修會花多少錢。

(C) 她想知道是不是男子把東西弄壞了。 　　　 (D) 她想知道東西是否還在保固期內。

6. 女子要那名男子做什麼？

(A) 留下聯絡資訊 　　　 (B) 三天後回來 　　　　 (C) 修理東西 　　　　 (D) 付維修費

Questions 7 through 9 refer to the following conversation with three speakers.

W: Hello, is this Great Wealth Bank, New Town branch?

M1: Yes. How can I help you?

W: May I speak to Mr. Watson, please?

M1: Hold the line, please. I'll put you through in a moment.

W: OK, thanks.

M2: Hello, Leo Watson speaking.

W: Hello, Mr. Watson, this is Sandra Davies. I'm calling to tell you about my job application for the bank teller position.

M2: Hi, Sandra. We're gonna make the final decision about whether to hire you.

W: Well, sorry to give you such short notice, but I've already found another job.

M2: No problem. Thanks for the notice. We'll remove your information from our job application list.

請參考以下的三人對話回答第 7 題至 9 題。

女：喂，請問是 Great Wealth 銀行 New Town 分行嗎？

男 1：是的，需要什麼協助？

女：請問 Watson 先生在嗎？

男 1：請稍候，我馬上為您轉接。

女：好的。謝謝。

男 2：你好。我是 Leo Watson。

女：您好，Watson 先生，我是 Sandra Davies。我打電話是想來跟您說關於我應徵銀行行員工作的事。

男 2：嗨，Sandra。我們很快會決定出是否要錄用你。

女：嗯，很抱歉這麼晚才通知您，我已經找到另一份工作了。

男 2：沒問題。謝謝通知。我們會把你的資料從應徵名單上移除。

7. 這段對話的主要是關於什麼？

(A) 工作的應徵 　　　　 (B) 服務的投訴 　　　　 (C) 政策的影響 　　　 (D) 刪除資料的方法

8. Watson 先生最有可能服務的部門為何？

(A) 客戶服務 　　　　　 (B) 風險管理 　　　　　 (C) 人力資源 　　　　 (D) 資訊科技

9. Watson 先生為什麼說「沒問題」？

(A) 他很樂意受理 Sandra 的申請。 　　　　　 (B) 他覺得他只是盡了自己的職責。

(C) 他覺得做這個決定很容易。 　　　　　　　 (D) 他不介意 Sandra 很晚才通知。

I. Warm-up

Proof of professional skills	Soft skills
A. C. F. G.	B. D. E. H.

Sophia Jones
前 BestTech 公司人力資源部副總裁及知名部落客

雇用合適員工的祕訣

能力好且充滿活力的員工將讓公司獲得成功，而雇用不合適的員工則耗費成本和時間。我希望以下的建議能幫助你找到合適的員工。

1. 招聘員工之前寫出清楚的職務說明。
   應微者光看某工作的職稱，可能不清楚這個工作的職責、必備條件和可能的待遇。因此，建議寫出一份詳細的職務說明來闡明工作內容。
2. 仔細查看履歷、求職信和證書。
   在招聘過程中，應該要有一張列表說明一名合格應徵者必須具有的關鍵特質。在檢視履歷、求職信或證書的時候應記得這張列表。這樣，你就可以淘汰那些不合適或不合格的應徵者。
3. 將軟技能納入考慮。
   雖然專業技能似乎是選擇合適員工的首要且最必要的標準，但軟技能也是你所該考慮的。社交智能、人際關係技巧、溝通技巧以及情緒商數都對團隊合作非常重要。

希望你覺得這篇文章有幫助，祝你徵才順利！

II. Reading

Scarlett Sky
喬治城 Mount State 路 156 號　郵遞區號 CA 98067
住宅電話：0141 294 5698　手機：07551 56977
電子郵件：scarlettsky412@tmail.com

10 月 14 日

招聘經理 Peyton Evans
LookFurther 設計公司
Hatfield 市 Delaware 路 58 號　郵遞區號 CA 98065

親愛的 Evans 女士：

我寫信是要應徵您在 helpfindjobs.com 網站上徵聘的行政助理職位。我按照要求附上了履歷、職位申請表、一般行政事務助理證書以及兩封推薦函。

在看過職務說明後，我確信我會很適合這個職位。我是個很有經驗又很有效率的辦公室行政人員。我先前擔任過四年多的行政助理。我精通各種辦公室套裝軟體，善於建檔、傳真、輸入數據、接聽多支電話線和回覆電子郵件等等。我對自己能處理多項任務和學習新技能的能力也深具信心。

我不怕提問，我也具有很好的傾聽和溝通技巧。我以前的同事們喜歡我的隨和與樂於助人。每當出了狀況，我一直是扮演問題解決者的角色，而非旁觀者。

我很樂意有機會與您見面，進一步談論我為 LookFurther 設計公司工作的資格。我真的相信我是這個職位上具有競爭力的人選，希望我能被列入考慮。請給我機會成為貴公司的助力。感謝您的考慮。期待聽到您的回音。

Scarlett Sky 敬上

III. Tasks

1. A	2. E	3. C	4. B	5. D

V. Learn by Doing

1. B	2. A	3. C	4. D	5. C

請參考以下的通知、文章和信函回答第 1 題至 5 題。

Hometown 書店

親愛的讀者：

非常遺憾，Hometown 書店開業逾五十年後，將於八月三十一日歇業。作為 Wood 鎮唯一的在地書店，我們很高興這數十年來一直為社區服務。在結束前一個月，我們會舉辦活動感謝那些支持我們的人，並慶祝我們的歷史以及對閱讀共同的熱愛。

Wood 鎮正在改變

隨著城鎮北邊的新購物中心開張，許多我們喜愛的在地商家已經熄燈。我們看到 Al's 披薩店和 Rosa's 烘培麵包店關門。現在，我們的老書店也遭遇到同樣命運。他們在今年夏日閱讀季結束後將關閉。我們這個城鎮裡所有美好的老東西似乎都要流失了。
我們知道 Clarke 市長重視新購物中心的經濟效益，以及它從鄰近城鎮吸引生意過來的能力。然而，她發覺到我們的社區精神是如何流失的嗎？有些東西是回不來的。我們的社區精神再也不會一樣了。

親愛的編輯：

我喜歡你寫的有關 Wood 鎮發生變化的文章。我時常在星期六的下午在我們美麗的小鎮的人行道上散步。我會吃個披薩、到老書店翻翻書，最後再加個奶油派結束一天。然而，事情已經改變了。我們的社區精神正在流失。

我知道我們不能阻止變化進行。不過，有些東西值得保留。如果我們的市長在發展地方經濟的同時，能找到一個保存小鎮歷史的方法，那會很棒。

Natalie Thomas

1. Hometown 書店關門最可能的原因為何？
   (A) 店主太老了。 (B) 生意被商場拉走。
   (C) 現在的書太貴了。 (D) 人們寧可看電影，不願看書。

2. 在今年的夏日閱讀季，Hometown 書店最有可能做何事？
   (A) 慶祝他們的歷史 (B) 成立讀書會 (C) 重新裝修書店 (D) 訂購新出版的書

3. Natalie 為何寫信給編輯？
   (A) 提議一個方案 (B) 應徵一份工作
   (C) 評論一篇文章 (D) 建議針對這個主題多撰寫文章

4. Natalie 週六下午最後造訪的可能是哪家店？
   (A) Hometown 書店 (B) Al's 披薩 (C) 新的購物中心 (D) Rosa's 烘培麵包店

5. Clarke 女士被建議做什麼？
   (A) 開一家新書店 (B) 關閉購物中心 (C) 保存當地歷史 (D) 停止發展在地經濟

英文文法入門指引 全新改版

Basic English Grammar Guide

呂香瑩 著

作者在多年的教學生涯中，深知學生在學習英文時所面臨的挑戰及罩門，因此編寫此書，介紹英文的基本文法概念，包括五大基礎句型、各種詞性與其用法，各種句型與其延伸應用。適用於英文初學者。

★十五個精心整理的章節，詳細介紹文法，從五大基礎句型開始，了解常見常用的句構，再進一步了解各種詞性的定義及用法，讓使用者奠定紮實的文法根基，釐清各種疑惑、提升英文程度。

12-3 分詞構句

分詞構句由**對等子句**或**從屬子句**簡化而來，可以表示時間、原因、理由、條件或附帶狀態等。

分詞構句的改寫方式與句型如下：

1. 由對等子句簡化而來：用於對等子句前後的主詞相同時。

Step 1 省略連接詞 and，加上逗點。

Step 2 若後句有主詞須省略；若有 be 動詞，一般也會將其省略。

Step 3 將後句的動詞改為分詞：

(1) 表示**主動**或進行意義的動詞改為現在分詞 (V-ing)；

(2) 表示**被動**或**完成**意義的動詞，一般將 be 刪去，只保留過去分詞

★實用的內容搭配情境完整的例句，希望讓讀者清楚了解用法。重點式的解析與即時的演練，幫助你破解文法上的難關。

✏ Try it! 實力演練

I. 填入合適的疑問代名詞 (who、whom、what 或 which)

1. _____ ate my cookies? They were here five minutes ago!

2. _____ has made you gain so much weight over the past few weeks?

3. _____ of these purses did Mr. Chen choose for his wife?

II. 依據畫線部份，以疑問代名詞造原問句

1. Helen lent her electronic dictionary to her classmate.

_____

2. The boy asked his father about the history of the church.

_____

3. The environmental pollution had made the residents suffer from various diseases.

_____

2-2-1 單數名詞與冠詞

1. 單數名詞與不定冠詞 (a/an)

(1) 以單字的實際音標來決定使用 a 或 an，而非由拼字決定。

	說明	範例
a	用於以子音開頭的單數名詞前	a **b**ook, a **ch**air, a **h**oliday, a **T**aiwanese, a **u**nique shirt, a **Eu**ropean [jurə`piən]
an	用於以母音開頭的單數名詞前	an **a**pple, an **o**range, a... **h**our [aur], an **h**onest ...

(2) 不定冠詞可以指「同類中的任一個體」，未限定對...

• The magician needs **a** volunteer to help him.

該魔術師需要一名自願者幫忙。 **Note** 指眾多自願...

> 將多種文法透過表格整理，希望化繁為簡，協助你綜合比較、釐清觀念。

2. 過去式動詞的變化

條件	變化	範例	
一般規則	字尾加 -ed	• look → look**ed** • help → help**ed**	• earn → earn**ed** • relax → relax**ed**
字尾為 e	字尾加 -d	• love → love**d** • care → care**d**	• move → move**d** • memorize → memorize**d**
字尾為 y：(1) 子音 + y	字尾去 y 加 -ied	• try → tr**ied** • cry → cr**ied** • study → stud**ied** • occupy → occup**ied**	
(2) 母音 + y	字尾加 -ed	• pray → pray**ed**	• destroy → destroy**ed**
「短母音 + 單子音」結尾的單音節動詞	重複字尾加 -ed	• stop → stop**ped** • drop → drop**ped** • beg → beg**ged**	• shop → shop**ped** • nag → nag**ged**
「短母音 + 單子音 [ə] 結...	重複字尾加 -ed	• prefer → prefer**red** • omitted → omitted • occur → occur**red**	• admit → admit**ted** • transfer → transfer**red** • transmit → transmit**ted**

❗注意

1. 主要子句與 as if 引導的子句為同時發生的事情時：**S + V + as if + S + were/V-ed**。
   • The patient felt **as if** her head were going to explode.
   這病人覺得她的頭痛得快爆炸了。
2. as if 引導的子句比主要子句早發生或已持續一段時間：**S + V + as if + S + had + p.p.**。
   • After an exciting game, these basketball player smelled **as if** they had not taken showers for a week. 在激烈的比賽後，這些籃球選手聞起來彷彿已經一個星期沒洗澡。

> **學習便利貼**
>
> 若無法判定主語和述語時，可先找出主要動詞。通常在主要動詞之前的字或字串就是主語，動詞及其後的字串為述語。

• Kylie has a sweet voice, and **so** does her sister.
  Kylie 的聲音很甜美，她姊姊的也是。
  Note 在此句中，has 表示「有」，是一般動詞，用助動詞 does 形成倒裝句。
• I have been to Scotland, and **so** has my classmate.
  我去過蘇格蘭，我同學也去過。
  Note 在此句中，have 是助動詞，用助動詞 has 形成倒裝句。
• Hannah is not addicted to Korean dramas, and **neither** are her friends.

> 規劃設計多種迷你單元，一眼抓住文法關鍵。利用簡單圖示比較掌握複雜的概念。

書與解析本與模擬試題不分售

111-80420G

三民網路書店
www.sanmin.com.tw